NO SIGNATURE

D1249316

NO SIGNATURE

William Bell

Doubleday Canada Limited

Canadian Cataloguing in Publication Data

Bell, William, 1945–
        No signature

ISBN 0-385-25379-6

I. Title.

PS8553.E55N6 1992   jC813'.54   C92-093534-6
PZ7.B45No 1992

Cover illustration Harvey Chan
Cover design Tania Craan
Printed and bound in the USA

Published in Canada by
Doubleday Canada Limited
105 Bond Street
Toronto, Ontario
M5B 1Y3

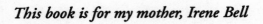

This book is for my mother, Irene Bell

ONE

I REMEMBER EVERYTHING.

My memory is like a dark cellar with long dim corridors that lead to damp gloomy rooms and in all the rooms hundreds of dust-layered file cabinets hold thousands of drawers packed thick with postcards; hundreds of scarred oak tables are stacked high with thousands of cob-webbed shoeboxes stuffed with postcards, each one holding a memory layered in a hologram of sound-sight-smell-touch-emotion.

And when I least expect it—maybe I hear a tune I liked a long time ago, I see a photograph of a far-away city skyline, maybe I just look out the window on a spring day and see a cloud going by on the wind—down in the cellar's murk a laser snaps on sending a reed of light searing through the darkness, reads a card, and feeds a signal into a coaxial cable that snakes through a maze of corridors, up the steep narrow staircase—and bang! the Replay surges into my mind, sometimes so powerful that it jolts everything else out of the way. And there I am, my skull invaded and captured by images and emotions I maybe don't want, but they're there and I have to look at them, feel them, even if only for a second, before I can turn off the volts and file the postcard away again in the gloom . . .

. . . like the time I was six, riding my new BMX bike, steering off the safe sidewalk into the forbidden territory of the road. I'd been trying since my dad had bought me the bike to pull off a walking wheelie, and that day I got up some speed, threw my weight back, not too far, and yanked back on the bars. And I found myself balanced perfectly, pedalling, front wheel in the air, and I thought, Wow! I'm doing it! So I looked around for an audience, someone to verify that I had finally mastered the walking wheelie, and that's when the rear wheel hit a stone in the road and the next thing I knew I was picking myself up off the road with a sore head and two bleeding elbows and I was suddenly glad there was no one around to see me fall . . .

. . . or the time a nightmare jolted into my sleeping mind and I wet my bed, waking up full of shame to the cold damp sheets and my mother said it's all right we'll just get a dry sheet, but I knew it wasn't all right. I knew good boys, normal boys, didn't wet their own bed. I knew if the other kids found out they'd laugh at me forever and I felt so bad, so scared the next night I did it again . . .

. . . or the day Hawk and I took a six-pack down to The Place, where the willows hung low over the creek where it met the lake in the big park between 13th Street and 20th Street and sat there talking about life while we watched the sails way out on the waves. After we finished the six-pack we walked giggling like grade nine girls to Tony Tattaglia's dad's barber shop up on the Lakeshore and I got my head shaved close, closer than what they used to call a brush-cut, and still under the sway of the beer we went to Hawk's house, and up in his room he numbed my ear lobe with an ice cube and prepared to jab a pin through it while he held a paperback novel behind it. Wait, I said to him, slurring my words, you sure you got the right ear? No, not your right, you dummy, your left, he laughed. Left is right and right is wrong. Now hold still, don't be a Jill. Be a big man, stick to your plan, he chanted, jabbing the needle into my flesh as I jeered at his lame rhymes. And after he finished, as I stood before his mirror, pleased at how tough I looked with my hair almost all gone and my left ear pierced, I said, Hey, Hawk, all I got is a bloody hole in my ear. He held up a small gold ring. Mom will never miss this, he said and I asked again, You absolutely sure you got the right—I mean the left—ear? I don't want anybody to think I'm gay . . .

. . . or the day I came home from high school and as I passed the front door on my way to my room I saw a card lying among some envelopes on the hall floor under the mail slot. But it was like the envelopes weren't there, all I saw was the card, a postcard lying face down with the address stamped on in black ink with one of those stamps you can get made up and the word DAD stamped on it too in the same colour of ink, nothing else on the card, no message, no signature, just the address and that word.

And down in the dark cellar the file drawers flew open, the tops burst from shoeboxes and cards spilled upwards into the air like upside-down waterfalls and the laser beam snapped on and went crazy trying to read all the cards at once as they floated to the floor, the laser jumping from card to card, sending millions of bits of messages buzzing along the coaxial cable, up the murky staircase into my mind. And I stood there in the hall that led to my room, rigid, as though the electricity in the cable was zapping me so hard it welded me to the spot . . .

. . . and what surged into my mind was the picture of a little kid that was me, almost eight years old, taking the worn lid off a Nike running shoebox and dumping all the postcards onto the floor of my room, all of them with my address and that one word stamped on them in cold black letters, me crying so hard I could hardly see, tears streaming over hot cheeks as I ripped each card to shreds so small they could have come from anywhere—all the while trying to think up the worst thing I could to say about my father. Jerk! Bastard! And still not satisfied because the words that came didn't begin to match the powerful mix of hurt and anger, hate and guilt, until in my rage I spit it out.

"I hate you!" I cried. "I hate you! I hate you!" . . .

. . . but then I managed to push that picture down again. I wasn't eight any more. I picked up the postcard, my hands trembling, my mind still fighting to stem the surge of memory Replays. Canadian stamp, postmarked Quebec City. I turned it over. Picture of a city skyline. I turned the card over again. In small print on the top left edge was the return address. I checked the stamp again. Postmarked five days ago.

Maybe he's still there, I thought, in Quebec City.

And if he is, I'll find him. And when I do, he'd better start talking.

TWO

IF I WAS GOING TO GO through with that crazy notion of trying to find my old man after ten years of silence, there were some minor details to work out, like how was I going to get away with skipping school for a couple of days? How was I going to get to Quebec City? Where was I going to get enough money? And the biggest question of them all: how was I going to get my mother to let me go?

After I'd made some tea and sat at the kitchen table for a while, looking out across our tiny yard to the row of ancient battered garbage pails that lined the fence to the right of our condo, answers started to come pretty fast.

I'd skip school and worry about the reactions from my mother and the vice principal later. After all, once you skip school you can't *un*skip it no matter what they do to you. I'd take the bus to Quebec City if I had to, but first I'd try to find the spare key to my mother's little BMW and get it copied.

The money problem required a bit more staring at the garbage pails, then I came up with something. My mother put money into a joint account for my education—she wanted me to go to university and be Somebody Important—but I couldn't put my hands on it. She's an accountant and she thinks that money was invented to be saved or invested. You didn't, according to her, actually *use* the stuff. But, I told myself, it was my money.

It only took a couple of minutes to find the passbook and chequebook for my account and a few more to find something with my mother's signature on it. I made out a cheque for cash for three hundred dollars, signed it, and then traced her signature onto it underneath mine. It wasn't really stealing, I kept telling myself.

I knew I'd have to sneak away without her knowing. She never talked about the old man and refused to answer questions about him when I asked her—which I hadn't done for years, once I got the message. If I told her I wanted to find him she'd throw one of her cosmic fits and refuse. She'd throw a super-cosmic fit when I got back, but by then it would be too late.

So I had it all worked out. All it took was a criminal mind and three cups of tea. I still wasn't sure *why* I wanted to find my old man, and I didn't feel like analyzing the matter, to tell the truth. Sometimes you've got to just go with your instincts.

I put my cup in the sink, threw on my coat and headed off for the health club to throw some weights around.

THREE

TWO DAYS LATER I had the three hundred bucks and my own key to the BMW. After my mother had left for the office—she usually takes the streetcar to the GO station—I wrote her a "don't worry and don't look for me" note and took off.

There was a light April rain falling and the traffic on the Gardiner and the Don Valley Expressway was thick, slow and stupid. I felt like I was surrounded by drugged-up escapees from mental institutions. But the BMW was easy to drive, comfortable, quick, with a sound system that would blow the sunroof out. Once I got out of the city it was kind of nice to crank up the tunes and drift down the road through the rain.

I reached Montreal at about three o'clock. If the drivers in Toronto were like mental deficients, the drivers in Montreal were totally schizoid, barrelling along, cutting in and out as if they were all trying to kill themselves before somebody else did. It took me almost an hour to make my way along the expressways and through the tunnel to the highway to Quebec City. By then a sky the colour of slate was trying to snow but managed only a few flurries.

It was near dark when I drove across the Pierre Laporte Bridge and the snow was coming thick and fast.

My stomach started to churn nervously as I got closer to where the old man was. I pulled off the road once I was across the St. Lawrence, gassed up and went into the little variety store next to the gas station to buy a city map.

I made my way carefully through the driving snow into the narrow streets of the Old City, crept down rue St. Louis, found rue Haldiman and turned right, holding on to the Bimmer as it fish-tailed its way up the grade. I turned off into an underground municipal parking lot, shut off the engine and immediately wished I hadn't come.

What the hell was I going to say to him? Hi, thanks for the postcard even though I waited ten years for it, now let's talk about how you ruined my life?

I sat there with my hand on the ignition, trying to decide what to do, knowing deep down I had to go through with this. Finally I got out of the car, grabbed my backpack and trudged up Haldiman, head down into the snowy wind. The ancient stone building stood silent at the corner of two narrow streets. The windows were dark but there was a dim light on over the door. I crossed the street and knocked, so nervous my throat went dry, rehearsing in my mind what I'd say when the old man opened it.

REPLAY

Back then, mornings were the best times.

I'd get up early, before Mom or Dad, and make my way downstairs, one hand on the wide banister, the other knuckling the sleep from my eyes. In the kitchen

I'd stand on tip-toe, stretching across the counter-top to turn on the coffee machine. Dad set it up for me each night. Switching it on each morning was my special job, and I never forgot. Then I'd pad into the family room and click on our little fourteen-inch TV, turning the volume down to zero. While the cartoons flickered silently across the screen I'd build with my Lego set. I had tons of the stuff. I could make boats, rocket ships, weird-looking monster trucks with strange machines mounted on them that could do anything my imagination came up with.

There I'd be, fitting bits of coloured plastic together while the coffee-maker spluttered and gurgled out in the kitchen, filling the air with the heavy aroma of strong coffee. Every morning I'd think, I can't wait till I'm old enough to drink coffee. I'll drink it strong and black from a thick white mug, just like my dad.

After a while I'd hear him banging around in the kitchen. I'd smell toast and hear cereal rustling in the box and hissing into the bowl. I'd go into the kitchen and show him what I was making, pointing out on-board computers, guns, or magic machines that could turn rock into gold or make bad guys disappear and transport them to horrible hot planets with no gravity or clean air. He always listened carefully to my explanations.

"You're gonna be an engineer," he'd say, "or a designer. Yep. You're creative, an artist." Then he'd laugh. "Just like your old man."

We'd eat our cereal, then have toast with Robertson's marmalade. I loved the sharp sour-sweet taste and dark orange colour of the jam, the shreds of bitter orange rind and chunks of ginger. Dad would listen to the news, talking back to the radio, making comments I didn't understand.

After breakfast he'd pour the rest of the coffee into his thermos, put on a fresh pot for Mom and stack our dishes in the sink while I got his lunch-box out of the fridge for him. Then he'd take a last sip of coffee from the white mug, slosh it around in his mouth and swallow with a huge *gulp!*, crossing his eyes at the same time. I'd laugh and he'd kneel down and hug me in his strong thin arms and kiss me goodbye. His face would smell of shaving soap.

He'd drive off to work at the tire factory and I'd pad back into the family room to watch more cartoons.

One morning I was sitting in a warm square of sunlight on the rug, building a boat that could convert to an inter-galactic space-fighter. The coffee machine had long since stopped gurgling and the kitchen was silent. I waited and waited for my father's footsteps.

Eventually, Mom got breakfast for me. She looked pale and angry and when I asked where Dad was she snapped at me.

"Just eat your breakfast and get to school," she said, throwing down a dish towel and rushing from the kitchen.

At supper that night I asked her again, "Where's Dad?"

"He's gone away," she said. I started to cry. "Don't ever talk about him again."

That night I lay awake for hours. Then I climbed out of bed, took up my Space Invader flashlight and stole through the silent house. In the bathroom I dried my eyes, noticing his sharp scent on the towel. I crept

16

downstairs, somehow knowing that the farther down I went, away from the safety of my bedroom, the less control I had over what was happening to me. I entered the living room and sat in my father's chair beside the little fireplace and turned off the flashlight, staring into the silent empty dark. There was a hole inside me like the dark, I thought, and it hurt.

I climbed from the chair and slowly descended the steep narrow stairs to the cellar, afraid. The air down there was damp and smelled of cedar wood. I had always liked that smell, but now it threatened from the darkness. I stood on the stair, holding tight to the railing. My flashlight beam seared like a laser through the dark cellar and picked out the curled cedar shavings on the cement floor around the legs of his stool and on the surface of the work bench where we did his sculptures and carvings. I played the light beam back and forth across the bench, looking for his carving tools and files and sandpaper.

They were gone.

FOUR

NOBODY CAME TO THE DOOR of the stone building. I knocked some more, then stepped off the narrow sidewalk and squinted against the snow, trying to see if any lights came on. None did. I peered through the slit between the drapes in the large window that gave out onto the street, but the room was too dark to see.

That's when I noticed the sign, *Appartement à louer*, in the corner of the window, and swore at myself. Then I thought, it wasn't necessarily his apartment that was for rent.

I adjusted my backpack, wondering what to do. I couldn't stand in the street all night hoping he'd come back—I'd freeze to death. The thing to do was rent a room somewhere and come back early.

I looked up and down rue Mont Carmel—not that I could see very far in the blizzard—and noticed a sign hanging out over the sidewalk across the intersection. I crossed over to read the sign: Auberge des Gouverneurs. The building was a lot like the old man's—block-shaped, built of stone.

The room they gave me was a corner garret jammed in under the sloping roof, the kind of place you just knew was described in the hotel brochure as a quaint *chambre* dripping with old world ambience. The window looked out over the intersection.

I dumped my pack on the floor, kicked off my soaking wet running shoes and stripped off my socks. I put the socks and shoes on the ancient radiator and hung my coat on the hook on the back of the door.

Then I turned out the lights and sat at the window as I chomped through three granola bars. The wind moaned and whined around the corner of the hotel and under the eaves. Across rue Mont Carmel was a small park, empty and dark despite the lamps that glowed weakly against the swirling snow.

Why was the old man in Quebec City? I thought. Then I asked myself, why wouldn't he be? He moved around so much you'd have thought he was dodging the cops or a credit card company. I looked down at the door to his building again. Maybe he wasn't here at all. Maybe he had moved on again.

I took a shower, went to bed, and dreamed I was in an old house running down endless corridors from room to room, frantically searching, searching.

REPLAY

Every day after school I burst through the wide glass doors, hopped on my BMX and raced home, pedalling like fury, flying down the hill, sweeping around the corner of our street, looking for his car in the driveway, hoping that everything would be all right again.

Then one day the first postcard arrived—from Montreal. It had a big picture of a church on it and my name and address stamped on the back. But no message. And no signature. Just DAD in block letters. My name and address and DAD were made with those rubber

19

stamps. I got a postcard almost every week after that, from Halifax, Vancouver, cities in the States, even one from Mexico.

Why didn't he say anything to me on the cards? I wondered. I wanted him to tell me what I had done wrong, why he left me, why we couldn't have breakfast together any more. Just tell me what I did wrong, I'd say out loud as I looked at the postcard, staring at that single word stamped in block letters, gripping the card so tightly it creased in my little hands. Tell me, so I can fix it. Tell me and I won't do it any more.

I saved all the cards in a Nike running shoe box, and every night before I went to bed I'd get them out and look at all the pictures from cities where I'd never been, crying, frustration and rage jamming me inside like floodwater surging against a cracked dam, hating and missing him at the same time, hating myself because somehow I must have made him want to leave.

At first I looked forward to getting the cards. Then, I don't know, they seemed to mock me. I didn't want them any more. I wanted him.

One night I carefully, slowly, ripped the postcards into small ragged pieces, so small nothing of the pictures or the printing remained, and stuffed the pieces into a supermarket bag. The next morning I took four more bags and poured my Lego pieces into them. I didn't want to be an engineer any more. I didn't want to be an artist like him. I took the postcard bits out to the road and dumped them into the sewer. Then, one by one, I carted the bags of Lego to the sewer grate, pushing the bright coloured pieces through the slots. They sounded like rain as they struck the water.

That day after school I didn't go home right away. I rode out to where the railway trestle crosses the Etobicoke River. I pushed my BMX along the tracks. The wide tires jumped and bucked on the ties. When I was halfway across the iron trestle, I shoved the bike over the edge, watching it fall as if in slow motion to splash into the muddy river.

When I got home my mom met me at the door and asked me a dozen questions at once. Where had I been? Why was I so late? Where was my bike?

"I hate him," I said. "I'm glad he's gone."

Not long after that the postcards stopped coming.

FIVE

I AWOKE TO THE WHINE of a vacuum cleaner in the hall outside my room. Realizing I had overslept—the story of my life—I jumped out of bed and took a look out the window. It didn't look much like an April morning out there. The sky was a hard porcelain blue. The wind of last night had carved long curved snowdrifts across the park and through the intersection, obliterating the sidewalks.

I dressed quickly, glad my socks and shoes had dried during the night, and went down into the street. It was cold but the sun hinted that the snow wouldn't last too long. There were no footprints leading to or from the old man's building. I knocked on the door. No answer.

After a sumptuous breakfast of doughnuts and coffee at a shop down rue Haldiman I trudged back, not too hopeful that anything had changed. I guess I was tired from my poor night's sleep and bitchy from the tension and frustration, because I suddenly found myself pounding on the door and cursing. Seizing the doorknob, I shook it hard, turning it as I cursed. The door swung inward.

How stupid do you feel, Wick? I asked myself. This is an apartment building, right? There's a sign in the window, *Appartement à louer*, right? You *could* have tried the door last night.

I found myself in a large dim foyer. There was a door to my right with a name tag over the bell button: Gauthier. Ahead of me, stairs. I took a deep breath and went up, gripping the banister to steady my hand. There appeared to be one apartment per floor, and the one on the fourth floor was empty. None of the name tags on the other apartments had the name Chandler on it.

Which meant my old man was gone.

Which meant I had wasted a lot of time, gas and money. Not to mention the hell to pay when I got home. But at the same time I was relieved.

I stared at the door with no name tag. Had he really lived there? Then I thought, there's only one way to find out.

It was easy to force the lock with my pocket knife, just like the private eyes do in the movies. The apartment was bare and lonely, washed with flat grey light. I took a quick look around. There was a galley kitchen, a small room with a stripped bed and a night table, and one large airy room with a couple of threadbare stuffed chairs. The painted floorboards creaked softly as I walked over to the window overlooking the Parc des Gouverneurs and the St. Lawrence River.

I caught the faint remains of a smell I recognized, and a Replay flashed through my mind. I looked around, searching the floor. There were a lot of gouges in the wood, as if someone had had a desk or table under the window. I got down on my hands and knees and peered under the radiator. I picked up a small wood shaving, curled in tight loops. I smelled it. Sure enough, cedar.

I looked out over the gently sculpted snowdrifts that stretched across the park. The tall old maples stood quiet, black against the snow and the hard blue of the sky.

The old man had lived here, all right. He had sat at his carving table and seen what I was seeing now. What had he done in Quebec City besides carve his little sculptures out of wood? Did he have friends here? A wife? Why had he come here? Why did he leave? And where was he now?

And why had he sent me that postcard after all those years?

SIX

I DROVE HOME THE SAME DAY. I won't go into the details about the greeting my mother gave me. She didn't know whether to be relieved that I was home safe or outraged that I had taken her car, made an "unauthorized withdrawal" from the bank—that's what she called it—by forging her signature and went looking for the ex-husband she never wanted to talk about. She decided to be outraged. I didn't really blame her. She made a lot of threats and asked a lot of questions that began with "How could you?" I figured my best bet was to look like I was sorry and not to argue, just wait until she ran herself down.

It took her a couple of hours. We were in the family room, sitting across from one another. The TV was on to a sitcom but I had pushed the mute button long ago, pretending to listen to her. Then her tone changed and I really did listen.

"Why?" she asked.

"I got a postcard from him. I thought . . . maybe he really did still care about me. See, Mom, when the postcards stopped coming, I thought he didn't care about me any more. So I wanted to go and, I don't know, say hello, see what he looks like now." I didn't add that I wanted more than that. Like explanations.

My mother was staring into her lap and picking with long painted fingernails at the nubbly upholstery on the arm of her chair. She took a deep breath and said softly, "You got others."

"Other what?"

"Other postcards." She cleared her throat. "He's been sending them all along. He never stopped."

"He never stopped? But—"

"Don't be angry, Stevie. I . . . I did it for you. I found them in the mail and threw them away."

"What do you mean, you did it for *me?* What the hell—"

"Don't you remember that day you ripped up all the cards he sent and threw the pieces down the sewer? You were so upset, it broke my heart to see you. After that I just threw them away. I didn't want to see you hurt again."

"So—now let me get this straight. He's been sending me postcards all these years, every month or so, like, he never stopped, and you let me think he did stop. And," my voice was real calm, "and you let me think that he'd forgotten all about me. My own father. And you did it for me?"

She sat there, her head down, linked her fingers together and squeezed. "I thought it would be better if you just forgot about him. Just put him out of your life."

"I *can't* forget about him, don't you see that? Just because you didn't want a husband you decided I couldn't have a father. I hate him sometimes, but I can't forget about him." I jumped out of my chair. "Sometimes I hate both of you!" I shouted as I ran from the room.

REPLAY

Hawk and I were snacking out at a doughnut shop on the Lakeshore one afternoon after school. Hawk had a passion for carrot muffins and every few days he'd tell me, "If I don't get a CM I'm gonna die, Wick," so we'd slip down to the doughnut shop and take care of his habit.

The doughnut shop was so hot inside the windows were steamed up. Not many people were there at that time of day; a bag lady by the window, munching on an oversized chocolate chip cookie, a lonely-looking salesman type wearing a trench coat over his suit, sipping coffee, a portable phone beside him on the table. We placed our order and took our food to an empty table, hanging our school wrestling team jackets on the backs of the plastic chairs.

"The Fanatic was a bitch today, eh?" Hawk commented, putting down his glass and wiping away a milk moustache.

"Yeah, he must have had a flea in his jockstrap, all right."

Usually Coach Leonard was a pretty good guy, but not that day. "You're wrestling like a bunch of geriatrics! The cheerleaders could kick your butts! Put some muscle into it, Richardson! Chandler, you move that slowly in a competition and you'll spend the match looking at the lights!"

"You know what I'd like to do?" Hawk said as he popped the last bit of muffin into his mouth. "I'd like to get some suds and go down by the lake and watch the waves for a while."

"Sounds good to me." I knew he didn't mean it. Hawk was death on drugs and alcohol ever since that time he got sick as a dog when we killed a six-pack and pierced my ear.

"Ah, the hell with it," he said bitterly.

"Take it easy, Hawk. The Fanatic was just in a bad mood."

The bag lady got up from her chair and shuffled to the door, pulling her thin coat tight to her neck. A couple of leaves blew in as she left.

Hawk was looking into his empty glass. "No, it's not him, Wick. It's . . . Do you ever wonder where your old man is?"

Hawk's change in direction caught me off guard. "Yeah, sometimes."

"Well, at least you know *who* he is. Me, I don't even know my mother's and father's names."

"Does it matter? I mean, the only people you remember are your mom and dad, right? How old were you when they adopted you? Three months or so?"

"Less than a month."

"So what's the problem? There was no relationship there. There's nothing to remember. No memories, no loss. Right?"

"I don't know. It's hard to explain. My mother gave me up right in the hospital. I don't know anything about her. Or about my father. All I know is that one of them must have been a real short-ass."

Hawk had made that comment more than once. He was a little sensitive about his height, even though he was pretty good-looking—straight black hair, clear pale skin. I hadn't known him as a little kid, but I figured he got more than his share of abuse from other kids. I also figured that was what got him into weight training and sports. Now he was muscular enough that you could tell, even if he had his jacket on, that he wasn't the kind of guy you threw insults at.

Talking about his birth mother like that, he set off some painful Replays in my head, scenes that played themselves behind our conversation the way images dance and weave behind a TV show when the cable isn't working and you've got two stations competing for the screen. I wondered what was worse, having memories that robbed you of sleep and hurt you like broken bits of glass lodged in the back of your mind, or having nothing except the knowledge that your own mother gave you away without looking at you, and that your father wasn't even around when it happened.

"I don't even know," Hawk's words broke in on my thoughts, "if they were married. Or if they lived together. Or any damn thing."

"Why not ask your mom and dad?"

"Don't you think I have? They don't know anything, either. The adoption people won't tell the new parents anything."

"You can find out, though," I said. "I saw a show on TV about it. You can go and ask the adoption people and they have to let you look at the records. You could search your mother out."

"Yeah, I guess. But I'd be afraid of hurting Mom's and Dad's feelings. So no matter what I do, I lose." Hawk laughed without mirth and shook his head. "You know, Wick, you take a guy like Leonard today, babbling on and on about commitment to the team, and responsibility. Those are his two most favourite words, right? Commitment and responsibility. 'You guys gotta learn these two things if you want to be treated as adults,' he says. I think he's talking to the wrong crowd, that's what I think."

"You and me both."

I got up and ordered another coffee and a glass of milk from the woman behind the counter. I took them back to our table.

"Maybe your mom and dad would understand," I said. "I think they would. They're pretty good that way."

"Yeah, you're probably right."

"So why don't you do it? Find out where your birth mother is. Go see her. Ask her about your father. I'll go with you. Finding your parents can't be that hard."

"I guess not. The thing is, though, I'm a little scared of what I'll find out. What if it's worse than not knowing?"

"Nothing's worse than not knowing," I said.

SEVEN

ROMEO WAS STANDING in a silver patch of moonlight in Juliet's garden, telling her, as near as I could make out between the thees and thous and wherefores, that he wanted to climb up the trellis onto her balcony, shove her into the bedroom and jump on her. But Juliet wouldn't shut up. She was yapping away so much that I knew Romeo would never get near her.

"O Romeo, Romeo! wherefore art thou Romeo?" she complained. What the hell was he supposed to say? "I didn't like the name Humphrey"?

Just as old Romeo started into another long hearts-and-flowers speech, a tinny voice from the front of the room cut in.

"Excuse me, is Steve Chandler present this morning?"

Ms. Cake, our English teacher, stood and pushed the pause button on the VCR, freezing Romeo with his mouth open. "Yes, he is," she said to the intercom speaker.

"Would you send him to the office immediately, please?"

Cake looked down the row of desks to me. "They've tracked you down, Steve. Away you go."

When I got to the main office the secretary told me to sit down and wait. It was at least twenty minutes before Mrs. Davis, the vice principal, came out of her office behind a scared-looking niner and, when the kid had left, she ushered me into her office like a stuffy head waiter in a snobby restaurant.

She closed the door behind me and I sat in the chair opposite her desk. She sat down too and began to look through the file in front of her.

Davis was one of those middle-aged women who thought they had to be tough or you wouldn't take them seriously. She dressed very severely—a dark skirt and jacket, white blouse buttoned up to the neck, a short no-nonsense hair-do. There were granules of make-up in the crow's-feet at the corners of her eyes.

She closed the file and looked up. Her voice was flat and her look was firm. Boy, was I intimidated.

"Where were you the last couple of days?"

"I wasn't here," I said.

She offered me a cold smile. "That is obvious, Steve. That's why I asked where you were."

My mother had refused to give me a note to keep the school off my back. She said I had skipped school and would have to pay the price. I wasn't going to lie about where I was. I wasn't going to say anything. It was none of Davis's business.

She gave a hard stare to scare me to death and waited for me to speak. I looked out the window at the cars moving down Kipling Avenue.

She gave in first. "Well?"

"Well, what?"

"Look, Steve. Let's not fool around. You were truant for two days. You're in deep trouble," she said in a tone that suggested I had just murdered all the janitors in the school with a chain saw. "Now, where were you?"

Teachers are really funny sometimes. Just because they think something is a big issue they figure you feel that way too. If they think you've committed some major crime like skipping school for a few days, they think *you* should be sorry. You're supposed to look contrite—we learned that word in vocab study before we started *Romeo and Juliet*—and you're supposed to feel guilty. The thing was, I didn't feel guilty at all. I was glad I'd gone to Quebec City, even though I went all that way for nothing, so why should I pretend otherwise?

But let's face it. I was an athlete and I knew a game when I saw one. I also knew how to play it. You didn't have to be a genius.

"I admit I skipped, and I'm ready to take the punishment," I said. "I had to go somewhere important, but I'm not going to talk about it." I gave her what I hoped was a hurt, I-need-understanding-not-discipline look. I had seen Hawk use that look a dozen times. He was a master at it. "It's . . . it's not something I can talk about."

Davis picked up a pencil and tapped the eraser end on her desk blotter. Her voice softened a little. "You're not in any kind of trouble, are you? Drugs, maybe?"

"Oh, no," I said. "It's something personal." Then I tried a line that always seemed to work on TV. "Please try to understand."

She tapped her pencil some more. "Okay, Steve. I'll go easy on you this time. One day's suspension."

The system made me laugh sometimes. I mean, Davis was sitting there at her desk with two framed university degrees hanging on the wall behind her, telling me that, as punishment for missing a couple of days of school, I was going to have to miss a day of school. Figure that one out. That's like saying the penalty for stealing a car was to go and steal another car.

But what the hell. I had a creative writing assignment due in two days, so now I'd have lots of time to work on it. I'd have to explain things to Coach Leonard, though. He was training me hard for a big invitational tournament in Thunder Bay in July and he didn't like me to miss practice.

REPLAY

After the postcards stopped coming I gradually got used to things the way they were. That's what little kids have to do—get used to things. They can't change anything. They can't control things or make things happen. Most of the time nobody asks them what they think or feel or want. Parents, teachers, others, but especially parents, do things, and the little kid's job is to adapt, to fit himself into a world somebody else made for him.

EIGHT

IT WAS A WARM SUNNY SPRING AFTERNOON. As soon as I came into the house my mother started shrieking. I was late. I had forgotten, hadn't I? Where had I been, anyway? I never thought of anyone but myself.

Well, I *had* forgotten that we were supposed to go to my grandparents' for Sunday dinner, but it wasn't like I'd been down at Sick Kids' Hospital selling crack to the patients. I had been over at Sara's working on a science report, which meant her doing all the work and me listening to tapes and talking to her. I dumped my books on my bed and headed for the shower. Fifteen minutes later I was ready to go.

"You're not going in *that*, are you?"

I was wearing jeans, a Rush T-shirt and unlaced high-tops. My mother had on a dark blue pant-suit over a white silk blouse with a red scarf at the throat. We didn't match too well. I didn't feel like an argument so I went back upstairs and threw on an old corduroy sports jacket.

When I came down again she was already out in the car with the engine running, smoking a cigarette. As she backed out of the driveway I turned on the radio. My mother immediately switched it off. "You know I can't concentrate on the road with that thing blasting," she complained, carefully putting the BMW into Drive. I slipped a Bruce Cockburn tape into my Walkman.

I knew my mother was nervous about going to her parents' place. She always seemed uncomfortable around them, as if she was still a kid trying to measure up. To tell the truth, I felt kind of sorry for her—when she wasn't driving me batty with her passion for making money and doing the right thing. She smoked heavily, chewed Rolaids as if they were candy, and went through a bottle of powdered organic laxative every two weeks. She hardly ever laughed. She was good-looking and dressed sharp, but never had time to date. She was skilled at her job—she was a partner in her accounting firm—but didn't know how to relax when she got home from the office. Her briefcase was always stuffed with extra work. She constantly worried about what other people thought—her colleagues, the neighbours, my teachers. When it came time for the cleaning lady to come, my mother would fly into a panic and tidy up the house so Mrs. Nadimi wouldn't think we were slobs. Who cleans up for the cleaning lady? What kind of logic is that?

We rode along through the Sunday traffic, me listening to my tunes, my mother gripping the steering wheel and glaring ahead as if there were terrorists out there aiming rocket-launchers at the car. Just once, I thought, I'd like to see her relax, loosen up a little, have some fun.

My grandparents lived in one of those neighbourhoods where the tree-lined streets never go in a straight line and are never called streets. They're all "lanes" or "paths" or "courts". The houses are big and dark, with leaded windows and perfect landscaping done by foreign guys in old pick-up trucks with their names hand-painted on the sides.

My grandparents came out onto the porch to greet us. Grandma kissed me drily on the cheek and led us into the living room, which was as big as a tennis court and stuffed with furniture you were afraid to sit on in case you got it dirty. Mom and Grandma had sherry, which Granddad poured form a heavy cut-glass decanter. He was working on something amber with a lot of ice in it.

The thing was, us sitting around like that, it wasn't like a family. You'd have thought my mother and I was business associates of my grandfather's or some art gallery boardmembers my grandmother had dragged home. Nobody told a joke or laughed or kidded. We all sat up straight and nodded politely and listened to our ice cubes clink in our glasses.

Then my grandfather stood. "Steven, come into the den with me. There's something I'd like to show you."

I followed him into what I always thought of as the brass, leather and walnut room—one of those really manly dens like you see in the movies. He showed me to one of a pair of leather wing chairs and we sat before a dead fireplace.

My grandfather is one of those guys who intimidates you without saying anything. I don't know what it is. He's tall—I inherited his height—but that's not it. He's rich, but that isn't it either. He just seems so *confident* about everything he does. I liked him a lot, though. Underneath, he was a kind man, and sometimes showed his sense of humour.

He'd been retired for a couple of years from a big insurance company where he had been a top exec. He was very conservative about everything—I could see him eyeing my jeans and T-shirt, and my earring drove him nuts—and, I hate to say it, a bit of a snob. He really believed that the rich and well educated—and white, naturally—were better than other people. "More substantial," he told me once. Yeah, right, Granddad.

I sat there, listening to the leather creak when I moved, and waited. I figured I was going to get a Talking To about something, and I didn't have long to wait.

"I understand you took a little trip, Steven."

"Yeah, sort of."

"Your mother was quite worried."

"Well, I left her a note."

He frowned and took a sip of the amber stuff.

"You took your mother's car." A strain of anger crept into his voice. "May I ask you what you were trying to prove with that little stunt?"

Why do adults always think you're trying to prove something? As if you couldn't just *do* something. I kept quiet for a moment, swirled my Coke around in my glass, looked into the cold fireplace. Tell the truth? I asked myself. Well, why *not* tell the truth? I had felt a little silly on the way back, going all the way to Quebec City and not finding anything, but I wasn't ashamed of what I had done.

"I went to look for my old man," I said.

My grandfather scowled. He knew that already. My mother would have told him.

"But why, Steven? That's what I was wondering."

"I just wanted to find him."

Granddad crossed his legs and, with his thumb and index finger, sharpened the crease in his pants. "You know, Steven, I hate to put it this way, but to all intents and purposes you don't have a father."

I shot out of my chair, spilling ice cubes and Coke on the rug. "Yes, I do!" I had never yelled at my grandfather before.

"Sit down!" he commanded in his boardroom voice. "Go on, sit!"

I did as he said, fuming.

"What I meant was, your father abandoned you a long time ago. What possessed you to try to find him? He clearly—I'm sorry to be so blunt, Steven—he clearly has no thought for you. What can you possibly hope to gain by opening things up again?"

"I don't know," I said. Actually, I did know, but I couldn't explain it. I knew he had never liked the old man, and had opposed the marriage.

"You ought to think things through a little. You worried your mother and you got into trouble—again— at school. You're a young man, now, Steven, you're not a child. It's time to start acting like a man. And a man acts responsibly."

Yeah, right, I thought. Tell me I'm a man right after you've tried to butt into something private, right after you've ordered me to sit down. How come when adults want you to do something they tell you you're an adult, but when they don't want you to do something you're suddenly not mature enough?

I let my grandfather talk. He was almost finished his lecture when there was a knock on the door and Grandma put her head in. "Dinner's ready, boys," she said, ducking out again.

We went into the dining room and sat at the long oak table. My grandfather said grace and began to carve a leg of lamb while Grandma spooned vegetables onto the plates and passed them down to him. All this spooning and carving and passing of plates went on in silence.

Once we had our food, Grandma tried to start up a conversation. The three adults talked about the weather and other fascinating stuff while I pushed my food around on my plate, pretending to eat. My mother told them about what was going on in the office and my grandfather gave her a lot of advice she probably didn't need or want. Then they all talked about the economy and my grandfather explained at length how the idiots in Ottawa were screwing it all up. I passed on the dessert, asked to be excused and went to the TV room to see what was on the tube.

My mother drove home carefully in the dark. "I'm sorry," she said.

"He said I didn't have a father," I said. "He had no right."

"You misunderstood him."

"You weren't there."

"He was only trying to help."

"That's no excuse."

That's how the conversation went. I was glad when we got home.

NINE

I WAS STRETCHED OUT ON THE COT beside our dinky little swimming pool one Saturday in June, catching some rays and dozing, trying to think up another excuse for not studying for my final French exam. I could hear the breeze from Lake Ontario stirring in the big maples along the foot of the yard, some little kids playing pick-up soccer out on the road, and the automatic vacuum going *kalunk! kalunk!* as it crept around inside the pool. I could smell the early summer odour of leaves, flowers, freshly mowed grass—somebody else's, not ours—and my coconut suntan oil. I had no intention of moving from that cot for at least a century.

My doze was interrupted by the *klop-klop* of sandals down the wooden stairs from our back porch and the *clap-clap* of the same sandals on the cement pool deck. Oh-oh, I thought. I kept my eyes closed, pretending to be asleep.

"Steve."

I ignored my mother, hoping that she'd go away. I wondered what she was doing home. Usually it was past six before she got back from work.

"Steve," she said again.

I turned and opened my eyes, squinting up at her. She looked formal and businesslike in a green dress pulled tight to her waist with a white leather belt. But her face was flushed, and she twisted her long thin hands together.

"I need to talk with you," she announced.

"I'm going to mow the lawn later, Mom, when it's cooler," I tried.

"It's not about that, although now that you mention it I would have been more than a little surprised if I'd found the grass cut."

"Aw, Mom, I just got comfortable. Can't whatever it is wait?" How come mothers never disturb you for anything *good?*

She pulled up a lawn chair and sat down. "I talked to your father today. On the phone."

I felt the shock wave right down in my bones. I sat up to face her, and said cautiously, "Oh?"

"It seems he . . . well . . . happens to be going out West soon."

I waited. I knew if I was patient she'd get to the point. The trouble was, it was hard to be patient. My mother always walks around a subject two or three dozen times as if she's hoping it will go away before she has to face it.

"He wants to take you to the wrestling tournament in Thunder Bay," she said.

"He does? But how did he know . . . When did he phone?"

She twisted her hands faster and looked out over the brown waves of the lake. "Well, I called him, actually."

"Really? You—"

"I got to thinking about what happened at Mom and Dad's, and I . . . well, I made a few calls and tracked

42

him down." The rest came out in a rush, as if she wanted to get it out before she changed her mind. "I told him that you were going to Thunder Bay to compete and asked him if he was interested in going with you. He said he would, and so . . . if you want to go with him, it's all right with me. I can get a refund on your plane ticket. If you don't . . ." Her voice died off as she ran her fingers through her short chestnut hair. Then she added quietly, "Maybe it's time you two got together again."

I tried not to sound too enthusiastic. "Sure, Mom, that sounds good. That sounds fine."

She rose from the chair. "Well, that's settled, then. I have to get back to the office." She headed for the stairs.

"Mom," I called after her. "Wait a second."

She turned.

"Why are you doing this?"

Her arms hung stiffly at her sides, her hands balled into fists. "I'll see you at supper," she said.

She fled up the stairs.

TEN

I WAS KILLING TIME AND TRYING to take my mind off things, doing wrist curls with my dumb-bells and watching a rock video by Steel Icicle, a new rock group from Vancouver. There was a half-dressed woman chained to a stake and a bare-chested guy was moving toward her, singing and thrusting the guitar in her direction. She looked like she was enjoying the whole thing and couldn't wait till he got to her.

It was a hot morning, the first Sunday of July, and a weak breeze pushed through the window screens into my bedroom. My suitcase was packed, I had checked my gym bag a dozen times—two singlets, the tight nylon bathing suit I used for a jockstrap, an old pair of Asics wrestling shoes and a brand-new pair of the latest model Nikes my mother had brought me for good luck, socks, soap, towels, everything I would need for the tournament and a lot of stuff I probably wouldn't.

I was wound up pretty tight, nervous about the tournament even though it was about a week away, but more nervous about meeting the old man. To tell the truth, I didn't know how I felt about the trip coming up, now that it was about to start. As usual, any thought about the old man brought a bundle of emotions and Replays with it. It would be easy to say I was excited about seeing him and that we'd fall into each other's arms when we met, just like Odysseus and his son in the Greek myth. But that was all a lot of crap as far as I was concerned. When people get hurt they feel guilty and mean and resentful.

Just as the next video came on I put down the dumb-bells, switched off the TV and stood looking at the framed photograph from the *Toronto Star* that had hung on my wall for a year.

REPLAY

My opponent for the Ontario High School Championship gold medal was a Korean kid named Jason Park from a school downtown. I had never been in a gold medal bout before and he had, more than once, I'd heard. I took one look at him and thought, "Oh, oh."

While I was getting ready Coach Leonard was yakking advice into my ear, but I didn't hear a word he said. I walked out onto the mat. I tried to calm my mind, to force out the roar of the crowd as they called out their encouragement—all for him, it seemed.

By the middle of the first round we were both pretty sweaty and tired. He had been ahead almost from the start but in the last moments of the round I managed to get a tight ankle lock on him and bridge through twice for four points, tying the score.

At the beginning of the last round he took me down right away. I escaped, but he was ahead again, and I knew I'd better go for it soon. We pushed, shoved, separated, tied up again, probing for weaknesses. Three times in a row, as soon as we tied up, I stepped back and as he moved toward me I dove for his legs. The fourth time, I made the move I'd been setting him up for. As soon as we tied up, instead of stepping back I flashed in close, forced my right arm under his left, dropped a little at the knee for leverage, drove my hip and thigh in tight, arched my back, and summoning every drop of strength I had, took a quick step to the side and heaved upwards, uttering a super-high-volume *'Aaaarrraaagh!'* As I hoisted him into the air I rotated, and I brought him down, nailing his back to the mat—a *Supplé*, the best I had ever done, so smooth it was like warm honey poured from a jar, so that he went down just like the books said he would have to. *Wham!* The air burst from his lungs when we landed, so I easily slipped into a head-and-arm, shoving his bicep over his mouth and nose. The ref was there, down on the mat beside us, right where he was supposed to be. His hand came up, he checked quickly with the mat judge on one side and mat chairman on the other, slammed his hand on the mat and blew his whistle. I jumped to my feet as the crowd roared.

The photographer from the *Star* had caught the Korean and me in the middle of the throw. I was proud of that picture. I looked at it almost every day. And I was looking at it when my mother shrieked from the kitchen, "He's here! Stevie! He's here! Hurry, so he doesn't have to come in and wait!"

As if she needed to remind me. She had told me a dozen times, "Make sure you're ready so you can go right out and get in his car. I don't want to talk to him. And I especially don't want him hanging around in the house waiting for you."

I went to the window. Parked in our driveway beside Mom's BMW was a white Volkswagen camper-van with maroon splotches all over it where somebody had been doing some body work. Now that the rock music wasn't pounding into my room from the TV I could tell the van needed a new muffler. One wheel cover was missing, and the lens on the left rear light was patched with silver duct tape. Nice wheels, I thought.

The rumble of the motor died and I heard somebody howling in Italian—opera music that got louder when the driver's door opened and my old man swung down onto the driveway.

At least I figured it was my old man. I hadn't seen him in quite a few years. He was thin and wiry, not too tall, with curly black hair. He was wearing faded jeans and a wrinkled white T-shirt. He slammed the door of the van and stood there, thumbs in his belt, and looked up at the condo.

I pulled back from the window, tripped over my athletic bag and fell onto the bed.

"Stevie! Come *on!*"

"All right! All right!" Man, was I tense.

I snatched up my suitcase and athletic bag and went downstairs into the living room. Mom was sitting in the leather armchair, watching her favourite soap, the hour-and-a-half Sunday version where they catch you up on everything that happened—or didn't happen—during the week. She was wearing wool slacks with a red silk blouse. She had her make-up on—she *always* had her make-up on—and her hair was carefully brushed.

She got up and hugged me. "Bye, dear. Good luck at the tournament. Bring home a trophy." She smiled.

"Okay, Mom, I'll try."

She walked me to the kitchen door, and as I struggled through with my luggage the phone rang. Mom grabbed the portable phone from the kitchen table.

"Stevie, wait, it's Hawk." She held out the phone.

"I don't want to talk to him."

A look of disbelief crossed her face. "What? I said it's Hawk. He wants to speak to you before you go."

"Tell him I've left."

"Stevie, what's—"

"I don't want to get into it right now, okay? Let's just say my so-called best friend and I have thrown in the sponge. He's not the guy I thought he was. Goodbye, Mom."

"But what should I say to him?"

"No message."

The door closed behind me as I walked out to meet my old man.

REPLAY

He would never admit it, but I knew Hawk had gotten into weight training and athletics for the same reason I did: he was trying to make up for his size. I was skinny and awkward; he was short. But unlike me, Hawk was a natural athlete. He could throw a football through the centre of the tire hanging from the maple in his yard with ninety per cent accuracy, and he caught even better than he threw. Guys on a baseball team feared him because when he fielded the ball from short he fired it so hard he practically knocked the first base man on his butt. No matter what sport it was, he seemed to have an instinct for the game.

"The only reason I don't play basketball," he once said, "is because of my ass."

I laughed. "What's your ass got to do with it?"

"Too close to the ground."

In wrestling, my height was a bit of a disadvantage because it slowed me down, but in spite of that it was the only sport where Hawk didn't leave me behind in a cloud of dust. We were in different weight classes, but sometimes practised together, and early on I discovered the real secret of his athletic success.

There was something in him, some kind of non-physical electric power, that was impossible to describe. It was as if he had a bottomless pool of anger, and when he wrestled he drew from it, the way a steel rod draws lightning from the centre of a storm.

Before a match he'd pace back and forth on the mat, so psyched he seemed to radiate a fierce energy that scared the hell out of most of his opponents before they walked into the circle. And when the match was on he moved in a series of explosions. He hardly ever threw a guy, but he racked up points relentlessly.

One time in grade nine I wrestled him in an open match. It was the only time he beat me. At the end of the match I told him, "You fight like an animal."

He laughed, and the next day at practice he sported a bright yellow T-shirt with GO ANIMAL across the front. From that day on, whenever the guys on our team wanted to encourage each other they'd yell, "Go animal!"

But I often wondered what was the source of that ferocious anger.

ELEVEN

THE OLD MAN WAS STANDING in the driveway by the camper-van, cracking his knuckles. When he saw me coming he stepped forward and held out his hand. It shook a little.

"Hi, Steve," he said. "How've you been?"

"Okay, I guess." I put down my bags and we shook hands. His grip was firm, his hands rough.

He looked me up and down. "You sure have grown!"

I could see myself in his face—the green eyes, the little bump on the bridge of the nose. I had inherited his black hair, but not the natural curl. He was thin, like I used to be, but I was taller than him now, and working with weights had made me heavier.

"Well," he said after a moment. "Might as well get going. You can put your stuff in here." He slid open the door at the side of the van.

I stashed my bags inside and he rolled the door shut. I pulled myself up into the front seat and caught the music full blast. I could never understand why people listen to opera. All the singers sound mad at each other and they're all trying to sing at once.

The old man hauled himself into the driver's seat, lowered the volume a little and turned the key. The rumble of the motor echoed all over the street as we pulled out of the driveway and lumbered up 23rd Street. I hoped none of my friends were around to see me travelling in a beat-up camper that looked like it had a permanent case of acne.

The inside of the van was messy and smelled of tobacco smoke. There were papers and matchbook covers all over the floor, along with a couple of empty beer cans. On a pull-out dashboard ashtray two pipes balanced dangerously. I turned to check out the back. There was a small fridge, a sink and a two-burner stove, and a table that you could swing out of the way when the van was in motion. Cardboard boxes and canvas bags were piled so high behind the back seat that I couldn't see out the rear window. The floor was littered with sawdust and wood shavings.

"You like campin', Steve?"

"Uh, I don't know. Never tried it."

"Oh. Well, that's what we'll be doin' for the next week or so." A few minutes inched by. "So, how you been lately?"

"Uh, okay, I guess."

"Doin' good at school?"

"Yeah, not too bad."

He finally gave up trying to make small talk and drove in silence. He swung onto the Queen E. and joined the Sunday traffic. All three lanes were packed pretty tightly—everybody out for a drive in the Sunday afternoon sun—but the traffic moved along past us at a good clip, as if we were a rock in the road. The old man had his window wide open. Good, I thought, the wind drowns out the opera.

The tape deck hanging on brackets under the dashboard was a good one. It could take both tapes and CDs, had a seven-band equalizer, programmable stations and as many buttons as a space capsule. All it needed was some decent music. I had my Walkman and a bunch of tapes in my suitcase, but I was afraid to ask him if I could play them.

I wondered why we were heading west along this highway when the way to Thunder Bay was north on the 400, but I didn't say anything—not even when, after about three quarters of an hour, he took the exit ramp to Hamilton.

We drove into the city and pulled up in front of a large building called Hamilton Place. The old man double-parked and yanked up on the emergency brake.

"If a cop comes along, just drive around the block and I'll meet you right here."

"I can't drive a standard."

"Oh. Well, it don't matter. I'll be back in a sec."

"Where are you going?"

"Tickets," he said, then he slammed the door and sprinted up the steps into the building.

I turned off the stereo and watched the traffic. After a few minutes he was back, breathless as he climbed in and started up the van.

"Got 'em," he said, and handed me two tickets to something called *La Bohème.*

"What's this?" I asked.

"*La Bohème* by Puccini." He sounded pleased. "It's only one of the best operas ever. I don't know if you like opera, but even if you don't, I'm sure you'll like this one. And the tenor is—"

"We're going to an *opera?*"

"I thought we'd start the trip off with a bang. I was lucky to get them tickets, too. You ever been to the opera, Steve?"

"No, I've never been to the opera. I can't say that I have. No."

We stopped at a red light. "You don't wanna go?"

"No, uh, it's not that. I just . . . sure, why not?"

"I can always take the tickets back."

"No, really, it'll be fine."

"Sure?"

"Yeah." What else could I say?

"Good. Check them tickets, will you, and make sure the date's right. I left the box-office too fast to check 'em myself."

"They're for tonight."

"And our seats are centre orchestra?"

"Right," I said, trying hard not to sound bored already. "We won't miss a thing."

We drove in silence for a bit. Soon we were rumbling through a park. The old man parked the van under a big maple at the shore of the lake, right in front of a sign that said NO PICNICS.

"Hungry?" He squeezed between the front seats into the back of the van.

"A little."

He reached up to release the catches on the pop top and then pushed upwards. The roof rose on a sharp angle, back to front, allowing him to stand upright. As he fixed the roof props in position I noticed again how thin he was. His ribs showed, his stomach was flat, his legs were thin. The only thing worse than a skinny guy in my opinion was a fat guy. There's no excuse for not being in shape.

When he'd got the top secured he swung the table into position and began to rummage around in the little fridge. He opened a can of beer, took a drink, and put soda crackers and a jar of cheese spread on the table.

"Mind if I take a little walk before we eat?" I asked.

"Sure. Take your time. We've got lots of it."

I walked along the lakeshore, glad to be away from the pressure. A few little kids were wading in the small dirt-brown waves that the light breeze pushed onto the beach. I sat down on a rock and leaned against the pole of a NO SWIMMING: POLLUTED WATER sign. I was thinking about telling the old man I had changed my mind and I wanted to go back to Toronto. My mother had cashed my air ticket but I could probably get another one. I didn't think I could stand spending the next four or five days trying to communicate with him. I realized now he was a stranger. Why would I have thought he'd be anything else? What did we have to talk about? What did we have in common? Opera? Yeah, right.

But then I remembered Hawk. If I went home, he'd call me every five minutes. I didn't even want to *think* about him, never mind talk to him. He'd probably start laying on the guilt, saying I had run off when he needed me most. Well, maybe I had, but so would anybody else who had just found out his best friend wasn't the person he'd pretended to be. I wasn't sure I was ready to deal with the new Hawk, or that I ever would be.

Anyway, it would only take a couple of days to get to Thunder Bay, I thought. A couple of days cooped up with the old man, making small talk, fighting ghosts from the past, insulating myself against Replays that would spark into my mind whenever I let down my guard.

I swore at nothing in particular and stared out over the waves. I noticed a wood shaving caught on the cuff of my jeans. I held it to my nose. Cedar. I must have picked it up from the floor of the camper. I flicked the shaving into the water and went back to the van.

TWELVE

THAT NIGHT WE TURNED UP at Hamilton Place for the opera. Oh, boy, I thought, won't this be great.

The old man parked the acne-van in the main lot alongside the Audis and BMWs and Legends. I had on my sports coat and a pair of light wool slacks, so I didn't feel too out of place. But the old man was wearing faded jeans ("Well, they're pretty clean," he had said back at the park), a white shirt under a leather vest, and moccasins that looked like they had survived the Battle of Frog Lake. He looked like Stompin' Tom Connors without the cowboy hat and boots, a little lost among the suits, jewelled tie pins, sparkling necklaces and costly dresses. I have to admit I tried to pretend I wasn't with him as we moved into the concert hall among the well-dressed crowd. He drew a few stares as he excused himself past people and sat down, holding his program with thick calloused hands. I was glad the lighting was dim.

After a few minutes, the music started. The orchestra conductor was one of those showy guys with long frizzy hair who flap their arms around a lot. He was really getting into it. Costumed rock singers were supposed to be outrageous but show-offs like him were supposed to be normal. Figure that one out.

The curtains opened and things got ridiculous really fast. A few guys were living in an attic somewhere in Paris. I got that from the program—I couldn't understand the Italian they were singing and I quickly got bored with trying to follow the English dialogue that was flashed on the wall above the stage. One character was supposed to be a painter, one a playwright, one a poet, like that, and they were starving and poor and cold, so cold they wore their long heavy coats and long woollen scarves indoors. Fine. The trouble was, they were all big fat guys who looked about as hungry as those overeaters on the antacid commercials who pigged out all night and wanted to get rid of the full feeling. And it got dumber. After they sang at each other for a little while all of them except the poet took off for a party or something. The poet was called—now get this—Rodolfo. He fell instantly in love with this Mimi babe who knocked on his door because her candle had blown out while she was climbing the stairs to her little room, and she couldn't find her key. She was about as good-looking as a basset hound. I mean, *nobody* except a blind man would fall in love with this one at first sight.

Mimi was supposed to be sick with tuberculosis (a lung disease associated with poverty, according to the program) and she was all bundled up under a heavy shawl, but she looked about as sick and starving as a quarterback. She was round and pudgy and she barged across the stage waving her thick arms all over the place. Plus, this weak tubercular babe had a voice on her that would knock down a hockey arena. She belted out her tunes, old Rodolfo shouted right back at her, and the first act ended with them in love. Yeah, right.

Well, it dragged on and on, and got worse, and I didn't pay much attention, not even when a horse ambled on stage pulling a carriage with a fat lady in red riding in it. She started shouting her tunes as soon as she lowered her carcass down from the carriage. I kind of wished the horse had crapped on the stage. It would have been funny watching the singers stepping around the horse-balls while they screamed love songs at each other.

The last act was supposed to be sad, but it was even stupider than the rest. Porky old Mimi was dying— which suited me just fine—and she was stretched out on a bed, propped up by pillows so her belly wasn't higher than her head. She looked like any minute she'd roll off the bed and bounce down into the orchestra pit. Mimi coughed every once in a while to show she was sick, but she was warbling away to Rodolfo, who looked like what he really wanted to do was go out with the other guys and have a smoke. It took her about eight hours to die. She finally flopped back onto the sheets and Rodolfo grabbed her chubby little hands and shouted 'MEE-MEEEEE!'— probably relieved that she finally croaked. The audience exploded into applause. Everyone around me was on their feet, clapping and shouting. I couldn't believe it. They liked that crap.

I looked over at the old man. He was on his feet pounding his hands together. And there were tears in his eyes. What a wimp.

I shrank back in my seat and pretended I was somewhere else.

Later on, when we were back at the van, he popped open a couple of Cokes and sat there talking on and on about the opera. I waited and waited but he made no move to get rolling. The parking lot was empty when I finally asked him where we were going to spend the night.

"Oh, we'll just put the top up and sack out right here," he said. "We'll get an early start in the mornin' and miss the traffic."

"We're going to camp in a parking lot? Isn't that slightly illegal?"

"Probably," he answered.

THIRTEEN

THE NEXT MORNING WE WERE ON our way while the sun was struggling up behind the eastern skyline of Hamilton, trying to burn a path for itself through the haze of pollution. The old man had made a thermos of coffee before I got up, and our first stop was a Tim Horton's near Hamilton Place, where we visited the washroom and picked up a couple of doughnuts.

The van grumbled through its broken muffler as the old man drove through the noisy streets and into the early morning crush on the Queen Elizabeth Way. He was dressed for travel—T-shirt, jeans, moccasins—and he hadn't shaved. Neither had I, for that matter. Parking lots are short on amenities.

Once we were headed north on the 400 the traffic thinned out. We cruised past Barrie and, at Waubaushene, picked up Highway 69, a two-lane that snakes its way north through rock cuts, forests and swamps. It was a sunny morning and the scenery in cottage country was sort of comforting—the blue of the lakes, the fresh greens of the leaves, the lighter blue of the cloudless sky. I began to relax a little.

And I have to admit it, the old man was an okay driver. My mother drives like there's a high-tension wire connecting her to the battery. She grips the wheel, hunches forward and makes all her moves in an erratic jerky manner. Going places with her puts heavy strain on the underarm deodorant. Not the old man. He sat back in the bucket seat, one hand on the wheel (which was covered with one of those fuzzy covers), the other holding his pipe, nodding his head to the music on the radio, or mumbling comments when the news was on. I gathered that he wasn't too happy with the way the Conservatives were running the country, or how the Toronto Argos' management was running the team. The van putted along, getting passed regularly because it wasn't too happy if it was asked to move faster than ninety klicks.

We didn't talk much. I guess the old man got the message from the day before that I didn't have much to say to him. I didn't know what to say to him. I wanted to get to know him, but I'd be lying if I didn't admit that I still held a lot of negative feelings toward him. And I still wanted to confront him about that day he disappeared from my life. Back when I was little, he was my favourite person, my hero. I didn't know what he meant to me now, but one thing I did know: he was no hero.

Early in the afternoon, a few miles north of Parry Sound, the old man pulled onto a side road that took us to Killbear Provincial Park. After paying the camping fee at the office, he got back into the van and said, "Look for site number fifty-eight." Then he drove slowly along a dirt road that wound through the bush.

"There it is," I said.

Our campsite was in a band of thick forest between the road and Georgian Bay. A picnic table sat in the shadow of a large silver birch beside a fireplace made of rocks cemented together. A well-worn path led through the trees to the water.

I climbed out on stiff legs and looked around, breathing in the fresh pine-scented air. The old man popped the top of the van, then popped open a beer. He got out through the sliding door and attached our permit to a clip on a post at the edge of the road.

"Nice spot, eh," he said.

"Yeah, looks good."

I walked through the trees to the lake and stood on a rock shelf that jutted out over the water. It looked cool, clear and inviting, deep enough to dive into. A small fish cruised by, its shadow following it along the sand bottom. The water stretched away from me for a long distance to a couple of small islands to the west. The place looked almost wild, except for the boat in the distance pulling a skier.

I returned to the camper-van to change into my swim suit. The old man was making a tee-pee out of twigs in the fireplace.

"Feel like some hot coffee or anythin'?"

"No thanks, I'm going to take a swim," I said, rummaging inside my gym bag for my swim suit.

"Good idea."

"How about you?" I offered, although I would rather have swum alone.

"Maybe later. What's that painted on the side of your bag?" he added. "I can't make it out from here."

"Nothing much. Just a nickname."

REPLAY

It was the first day after Labour Day and the yard of 20th Street School was packed with a moving sea of bodies.

Cars slipped in through the gate in the chain-link fence and kids got out reluctantly, feeling a hundred pairs of eyes burn into their backs as they turned and reached into the cars for new back-packs. Other kids filtered in on foot.

Little kids hung back, checking out the big kids to see how they themselves should act. New kids stood off by themselves like rabbits caught in a car's headlights on a dark country road. The grade eights formed their own exclusive groups, far from the school doors, ignoring the lesser beings in the school yard. They didn't talk to anyone below grade seven, would only share their attention with teachers, and then only a select few of them. They pretended to be bored but excitement buzzed in their conversation. They greeted kids they had talked to half an hour ago on the phone like they hadn't seen them all summer.

The guys were gathered in bunches, acting tough, swearing, punching each other, laughing in cynical bursts as their eyes scouted possible victims for derision. A few of the ones with confidence were putting the move on girls with hard clever talk, standing with their hands in their pockets. The girls, pleased with the attention, either laughed at everything the boys said or rolled their eyes, feigning boredom.

Other girls in chattering flocks pretended to admire each other's new clothes or aimed sharp cruel remarks at the outsiders who wore clothes from the discount department stores along Lakeshore Boulevard.

I was a grade eight too, but not with the right crowd. Not with any crowd. I was a wall-crawler. I leaned against the rough red brick of the school, stiff with anxiety, looking around, hoping no none would notice me. I had on new deck shoes, jeans and the right kind of shirt, but none of that was enough to get me into the inner circle. I couldn't make quick jokes. I was way above average height but way below average weight, skinny and lanky, like a collection of sticks held loosely together with string. I had limp black hair and a rash of acne that flared and reddened when I was embarrassed. I seemed always to be embarrassed.

When the bell rang the little kids surged toward the door, forming a noisy unruly line-up. We hung back, trying not to look eager, but the truth was we were bored with summer and we wanted to take up our role as kings and queens of the school. At least, those who could pull it off.

In the line-up at the school door I noticed a short kid I hadn't seen before. A new back-pack was slung over his shoulder. Probably jammed full of new notebooks and throwaway ballpoint pens, felt-tip markers, maybe a set of coloured pencils. Just like my pack. He stood quiet and calm, but his eyes flitted from face to face.

We filed down the noisy hall and into our classroom, first kids in taking up the desks at the back. Smell of chalk and new paint and paste and that unidentifiable school smell that hung like invisible smoke in every room. The teacher was Mrs. Roper. She had been my teacher once before and she looked like she was wearing the same flower print dress she had on when school let out last June. Same hair-do, long and turned up at the ends, same thick-soled shoes. Everything about her was thick too, her neck, her arms, her waist, her legs. She taught social studies and phys ed, and she was to be our home-room teacher.

She welcomed us back and started reading off the roll, smiling at each kid as they acknowledged their names. There were three new ones, two girls and the short guy, who was sitting in front of me. When Mrs. Roper finished taking attendance she told us we would have the first lesson. History, she said. Our own history, she said.

"Most people don't realize," she began, "that our names—at least in English—come from places, occupations, or objects." Roper talked to kids as if they were imbeciles or about six months old. She smiled and looked around as if a blinding light was supposed to shine in our skulls at this wonderful revelation. "For example, Eileen Ford."

A girl across from me—one of the new ones— turned red as her eyes widened.

"Your surname," Roper went on, "is taken from a place in a river where it's easy to cross. A ford. That's a place. Can anyone think of another surname that comes from a place?" She looked around.

This was the time for the eager types. Every class had a few and they always tried to stake out their ground on the first day so the teacher could find out right away that they were good students. Most of them were girls.

"Lake?" one of them offered. "Rivers?" said another. "Stone!" asserted a third.

"Good," Roper beamed, "very good. And some names come from occupations. Like yours, Amy. You all know what a blacksmith is. Well, Amy's last name, Smith, comes from that occupation. Who can think of another?"

The eager types chimed in again. "Carver," said one. Then a voice boomed from the back row. "Yeah, I guess Ramjit's family used to be rock stars."

The room was quiet for a second. Roper stared at Tony Tattaglia, mystified.

"Singh, get it?" Tony added.

Laughter. Ramjit's large brown eyes widened and he turned on an embarrassed smile. Roper's face clouded as she glared at Tony. He had been in my class every year since grade two and he got in more trouble each year. He was always shouting out his jokes in a loud deep voice that made it sound as if he talked in capital letters. Mostly we liked his disturbances because he was pretty funny, and even when he wasn't he got into trouble and that was even more entertaining than his funnies.

Roper ignored him. She looked at me. "One of the most interesting cases is yours, Steve."

I felt the needle-points of all the eyes in the room and a hot flush crept up my neck and into my face. I felt conscious of every zit.

"Your name, Chandler, comes from candle-making. Candle-makers used to be called chandlers, not candlers, and before we had electricity that was a very important job, because candles were the only way people could provide light for their houses." She smiled. "So you're a candle-maker."

Tony shouted, "'He's so skinny he ought to be called *WICK!*'

Laughter rolled through the room like a tidal wave and crashed around my head. I stared at my hands clenched on the desk.

"Wick!" "Wick!" Roper cut off the laughter and tried to regain control of the class. All around me the whispers hissed. "Wick!" "Wick!"

At lunch I left the school and crossed the yard as

fast as I could, heading for the street. Behind me I heard, "Hey, Wick, better get your mother to feed you some more!"

"Yeah, Wick, go to Weight Watchers and do everything backwards!"

After that, nobody except teachers and my mother called me Steve. I guess some kids get used to nicknames, but every time someone called me Wick I cursed that bone-headed teacher and her equally bone-headed lesson about surnames.

Hated it until the short kid who sat in front of me became my friend.

Which was surprising, because he was Mr. Athlete, always in the centre of a cloud of dust thrown up by a fast-moving pack of guys kicking, hitting or tossing a ball around the school yard. Me, I was never anywhere near the dust. I'd be on my own, waiting for the bell. But in class he would often turn around and ask me questions about the work we were doing.

One time he called me Wick and I freaked at him so loud Roper had us both in at recess to tell us about good manners in class. When she finished her lecture and left he asked why I was so strung-out about my nickname.

"Because it's stupid and I hate it," I said.

"Relax," he said, "it's no big deal."

"Not for you. You're not skinny, and your nickname's okay." It was true. He was called Hawk. Nobody knew why.

"You hate the name or you hate being skinny?"

I hadn't thought about it, but he had a point.

"Being skinny."

"Nobody has to be skinny if they don't want to. Meet me after school. I've got something to show you."

After the bell went we tore out of the school yard and headed down 20th Street to the Lakeshore. Hawk took me way down near 35th Street to a health club called Alterations. It was part of a chain I saw advertised on TV all the time, with sleek-looking women in skintight body suits telling us if we came to the club a few times a week the universe would change direction. Or men in cut-offs and T-shirts with the arms ripped out, flexing and acting tough.

Turned out Hawk's dad worked there afternoons. There was a big weight room with all kinds of free weights, benches and a mammoth Nautilus. There were electronic programmable stationary bicycles and rowing machines. And saunas and whirlpools, the whole works. Because afternoons were the slow time, Hawk's dad let us work out there after school.

So I started weight training. Almost every day. Hawk showed me the routines and his dad told me what to eat. "You got to take in tons of protein when you weight train," he said. And gradually, slowly, my skinniness went away. My chest was more than a bag of bones, my arms touched the cloth on the sleeves of my shirts, my legs didn't look like paddle handles. By the time I made grade nine at Lakeshore Collegiate I was pretty well built, or at least well on the way.

And I didn't mind being called Wick any more. In fact, I kind of liked it.

FOURTEEN

I SPENT THE AFTERNOON ON THE ROCK by the water,
swimming and reading a thick novel called *Shogun*. The
old man came down for a while and splashed around like
a wounded duck. Seeing him in his bathing suit, I
realized he wasn't so thin after all. His muscles were small
but knotty and wiry, like cables—the way a guy gets
when he works but doesn't do weights. He still looked
pretty wimpy, though.

Later on in the afternoon, while the old man was
cleaning the acne-van's spark plugs, I put on my trainers
and took a half-hour run along the dirt road that twists
and turns through the park. I jogged along just fast
enough to keep ahead of the mosquitoes and blackflies
that hovered in the shady areas looking for tourist blood.
It was a pretty big park, although there weren't many
campers—just a few families and a couple of RVs with
old people sitting outside in lawn chairs reading the
paper. When I got back to our campsite I took a last
swim and dressed.

By that time the old man had a small fire going in
the fire pit beside the picnic table and there was a pot of
stew and a coffee pot sitting on the rocks at the edge of
the flames. I didn't know why he cooked on a fire instead
of the stove in the van and I didn't ask.

After dinner, as it grew dark and cool enough to keep the bugs down, we sat beside the fire and the old man opened another beer and started asking me all kinds of questions about school and stuff like that—the kind of questions asked at Christmas time by aunts and uncles you haven't seen for a year or so. I answered him as best I could without telling him anything personal. I tried to work up the nerve to ask him something about himself but I failed. The time didn't seem right.

Then he started asking about Mom. He was fishing around with small talk but I knew what he was after. Finally he got to the point.

"Does she go out much?"

The truth was, she didn't go out at all, unless it was some office party. As far as I knew she had dated twice, maybe three times while I was growing up, but the guys never showed up again.

When I got older I wondered about it. I mean, my mother wasn't a beauty queen but she was pretty good-looking. And she always dressed well, never made a move without her make-up on. But no men in her life. I knew she must have been lonely. Just then I felt a twitch of guilt. Maybe it was me that was holding her back. Maybe she gave up men because, with me and her job, she didn't have time.

"No, she's pretty busy," I said.

"Yeah, she's done okay for herself."

"She sure has. She's the top accountant for the company. She also made some money on the stock market; she's pretty smart that way. That's when she bought the condo."

"Nice car she drives, too."

I caught a tone in his comment that I didn't like. "Well, why not? She earned it," I said.

"Course she did. But she never had no steady guy, eh?"

"Not really."

"Too busy, like you said."

"Yeah."

The old man looked into the fire for a moment. Then he took another pull on the beer can and said, more to himself than to me, "Maybe nobody can meet her standards."

"What the hell's that supposed to mean?" I snapped.

"Nothin'. Forget it. I was just talkin' to my—"

I stood up. "I'm going to bed."

He gave me an apologetic look and nodded. "Okay. 'Night."

I climbed into the top bed, took off my clothes and got into my sleeping bag. I wasn't tired but no way was I going to sit there and listen to him talk about my mother like that. Maybe I had to travel with him but I didn't have to take any crap from him.

He stayed at the fire for a long time.

REPLAY

Hawk and I called his house the United Nations because his dad was half-black, born in New York, his mom came over from Viet Nam when she was four, and Hawk was a short white kid from who-knows-where.

I liked it at Hawk's house. His parents were low-key, easygoing types. They published a local weekly newspaper called *Good News*, which they started up when Hawk was little because they were sick and tired of all the gloom-and-doom, wars and disasters and dirty politics of the major papers. Hawk's parents figured more good things happened in the world than bad things but we never get to hear about them. *Good News* contained only positive stories, like fund-raising campaigns for the Queensway General Hospital, scholarships won by local students, environmental stuff and a Citizen of the Week citation. I sort of agreed, but, to tell the truth, the paper was a little boring. Maybe that was why it didn't bring in much advertising revenue and Mr. Richardson had to work at the health club. Mrs. Richardson, a small thin feisty lady, wrote most of the stories.

Hawk's house was the opposite of ours. My mother and I got along okay most of the time, but our house always seemed to have an atmosphere of tension. I remember reading a story called "The Rockinghorse Winner" where this little kid named Paul thought he heard voices coming out of the walls saying, "There *must* be more money; there *must* be more money." I'm not saying our place was that bad, but, like I've said before, my mother's two big goals were making lots of money and keeping up appearances. Our new condo was carpeted everywhere and full of costly new furniture that didn't look very inviting. In the downstairs bathroom were vases of dried flowers and baskets of little rose-shaped soap cakes on the back of the toilet beside the can of aerosal air-freshener. Is that pretentious, or what?

Hawk's house was calm and comfortable. The dishes didn't match, the furniture was worn, and the rugs were threadbare. There was nothing fancy or put-on about his house or the people who lived in it. I guess that was why I spent so much time there—that and the fact that Hawk was my best friend.

FIFTEEN

THE DEAFENING CHIRPS of a thousand excited birds woke me up the next morning to the smells of frying bacon and fresh coffee. I wasn't supposed to like either one of them—Coach Leonard's orders—because coffee does all manner of subtle damage to the body and bacon contains nitrites, which are bad too, but I forget why.

Coach Leonard was totally rabid about all that stuff. He looked it, too. He was small, muscular, wore his hair super-short and had a hard single-minded stare. That's why we called him the Fanatic. I'd hate to have faced him on the mat. He once told me that when you grow up Jewish in a Gentile neighbourhood in Toronto you get tough or you get beaten up a lot.

He demanded a lot from us and he was always preaching about proper diet as well as proper training. Hawk had been converted long before—his parents had always been granola and alfalfa-sprout types—except for his carrot muffin habit. I followed the Fanatic's regime. I had to if I wanted to stay on the wrestling team and, besides, I thought he was right.

I rolled over in the bunk and stared at the camper's slanted ceiling, letting my nose enjoy the forbidden aromas. The more I thought about it, the more I realized everybody I knew was paranoid about what they ate. My mother was always on one kind of diet or other, the water diet, the banana diet, the no-protein total-carbo diet, the non-carbohydrate total-protein diet. Last year she joined one of those weight-loss support groups and came home every week drowned in guilt. The thing is, she wasn't fat and never had been.

And a lot of the girls at school got totally boring about the whole thing. My friend Sara was always saying, 'I'm so *fat!*' as if she could hardly get through the door. She looked just fine to me. All the girls seemed to be dieting. They'd rather have been dead than overweight. They all wanted to look like those flat-chested concentration camp types that model in magazines. They wanted to be hangers—that's what they called models. Even when Sara's best friend checked into the hospital with a case of anorexia and almost died, Sara said to me she secretly wished she could be anorexic for a few months so she could get her weight down.

"Down to what?" I had asked her. "Who wants to go out with a bag of bones?"

She told me I didn't understand. Right on, Sara. Go forward three spaces.

Anyway, I didn't want to lie there any longer thinking about Sara, so I crawled out of the sleeping bag, pulled on my damp bathing suit and went down to the lake. The old man was standing by the calm green water, leaning against a thick birch, barefoot, bare-chested, looking out toward the islands. He didn't have a beer in his hand or his pipe in his mouth, so I figured he hadn't been up long.

I felt uneasy about last night and tried to think of something to say to smooth things over.

He beat me to it. "Nice day, eh?" He tore a loose piece of bark from the birch and began to work it with his hands like a piece of leather.

"Yeah, great. Coming in?"

"Nope. Had my dip already."

"Oh."

I dove in and started to stroke out toward the horizon.

"Don't go out too far," he shouted after me. "Breakfast is ready."

Soon we were on the road again. It looked like another great day, and except for the pipe smoke and the horrible music—country and western this time—I half-enjoyed myself.

We continued north on 69 under a blue sky decorated with slow-moving ice-cream clouds that broke the sun's glare every few minutes. I caught the odd glimpse of Georgian Bay on the left before we swung inland and crossed the French River on a big silver trestle bridge. We made Sudbury about ten and the old man took the turn-off into town.

"Have to buy some food," he said.

Coming into Sudbury is like coming into any town, I guess. You have to drive past all the junk-food places—hamburgers, a million flavours of ice-cream, pizza, chicken massacred in various ways, fish and chip stores that always look like they're about five minutes from bankruptcy—and then the malls with huge ugly signs and parking lots that stretch on forever. The buildings in Sudbury seemed to be carrying on a losing fight with the ugly black rock that poked up everywhere through the thin soil.

The old man turned in to a little mall and parked the van between two pick-up trucks in front of a store.

"I thought you wanted groceries," I said.

"Right." He looked hesitant as he shut off the motor.

"This is a *drug* store." I pointed to the big sign with I.D.A. painted in red half-metre-high letters on a white background. "You want the IGA, right?"

"Oh. Oh, yeah. Pretty stupid. Guess my mind was somewhere else."

The old man started up the van and we drove around some more. He stopped three times to ask for directions, looking for a food store, squinting through the windshield like a pensioner. Finally he pulled into another mall where there was a little IGA store.

"You don't need to come in," he said. "I'll only be a sec."

"I think I will. I'd like to stretch my legs."

Big mistake. I thought shopping with Mom was frustrating. The old man grabbed a cart, one with a wheel that flapped like a demented sparrow, and walked to one side of the store.

He moved up and down the aisles, squinting at the cans, bottles and bags lined up on the shelves, as if he was trying to memorize all the labels. After about ten minutes I said, "What are you looking for, anyway?"

"Oh, soup, stew, like that," he said vaguely.

"Is there something you want me to get, maybe save some time?"

He was dropping cans with big coloured pictures of stew on the labels into the cart. "No, it's okay. I think of things I need as I go along. Why don't you wait outside in the van? I won't be long."

He seemed anxious to do his shopping without me around, so I figured fine, he wants to be alone, that's okay with me. He came out about half an hour later, weighed down by shopping bags, just as I was ready to die from boredom.

After a quick stop at the beer store, which he found easily enough, we were on the road again, rumbling past the slag heaps and the pinkish granite rocks that stretched away from the highway toward the big chimney that dominates the city.

Once out of Sudbury we were heading into the afternoon sun. We drove for over an hour, through towns with fascinating names like Whitefish, Massey and Spanish, before the old man took a right onto a secondary road. Not far along he turned into another campground, this one called Chutes Provincial Park. I knew from my four years of totally boring French classes that a *chute* is a waterfall, so I figured this might be a pretty spot. Sure enough, as soon as the old man pulled into a campsite and the rumble of the broken muffler died away, I could hear the falls.

I got out, stretched the kinks out of my back and followed a path through a stand of evergreens toward the distant roar, waving the bugs away as I walked. The path opened onto a small sand beach on a tiny lake—more like a pond—of slow-moving dark water flecked with foam. The shore opposite was lit up by the afternoon sun. At the far end of the pond was a small waterfall gushing over a rock shelf. At the nearer end the pond narrowed into a small river that rushed away into the bush.

I went back to the van and put on my bathing suit. The old man was brewing up some coffee on the stove, puffing on his pipe, filling the van with foul-smelling smoke, and humming to himself. I headed for the pond.

Under my feet the path was cool and damp, covered with pine needles that made walking soft and silent. I waded into the pond carefully because the water on this side was shaded and dark, making it hard to see the bottom. I pushed off, gasping as the cold water enveloped me, and swam toward the falls. The current was surprisingly strong, but not threatening. The sun on the foaming water of the falls turned it milk-white as it thundered into the pool. I swam against the current and pulled myself up to lie on a flat rock next to the falls. The sun against my back felt good. There's something about water and sun that usually opens a tap and drains all the tension out of me. Not this time, though.

My mind returned to my old man. I already dreaded sitting around with him during and after supper with nothing to do except read my book. Then after dark, what? Go to bed at nine o'clock and lie there staring at the ceiling like last night?

Maybe I'd ask him about himself. But now I wasn't sure I felt like going into all that. He'd start digging up the past, and I wanted to do anything but. Why open it all up again? It was over.

Except I wasn't doing a very good job of forgetting.

I gingerly lowered myself into the cold water. As I struck out I noticed the old man on the far shore, turning and taking the path back to the campsite. He had been watching me.

We had supper in silence, mostly because I brought my novel to the table and read while I ate so I wouldn't have to make lame conversation. The meal was stew mixed with pork and beans. I hated to admit it, but the stuff didn't taste too bad. After we had eaten, the old man chopped up some firewood while I did the dishes. He said it was a nice night for the fire, and besides, it would keep the bugs away.

I was sitting across the flames from him in a lawn chair, struggling to read in the waning light. He was on his third beer. He had peeled the bark off a thick stick and was carving grooves and shapes into it with his pocket knife. The little fire popped and crackled every once in a while—because he was burning hemlock, he told me.

"Mind if I ask you somethin'?" he asked, tossing the stick into the fire and folding up his knife.

I looked up from *Shogun*, but held it open. "Yeah?"

"What's eatin' you, anyway?"

"What do you mean?"

He stuffed the knife into his hip pocket. "You know what I mean."

"No, I don't." I looked down at the page.

"That. Just like that."

I looked up again. His mouth was set in a firm line. He drained his beer and dropped the can beside his chair. He pulled his pipe out of the pocket of his bush shirt, and pointed the stem at me.

"I'm tryin' to talk to you and you look at your book. That's good manners, is it?"

"Sorry," I said. I closed the book and stared at

the flames. They were orange-yellow-red, but blue where they separated themselves from the whitened ash of the wood. I waited.

"What's the problem that you can't at least be polite? I mean, okay, we haven't seen each other for a long time. I know it hasn't been easy for you. But I've waited a couple of days. You're not just shy, you're rude."

Rude. That was the kind of word my elementary school teachers used.

"Can't you talk to me?" he went on. "I was hopin' we could be . . . I don't know . . . friends."

Yeah, right, I thought. You turn up from out of nowhere and all of a sudden we're pals.

"Well?" he said, his voice edged with anger now.

"Well what? What do you want me to say? This wasn't my idea, this trip. I didn't even want to come," I said.

"Why did you then?"

"Mom made me."

He got up out of the lawn chair and got another beer out of the fridge. Great, I thought, maybe he'll leave me alone. I opened my book. No such luck.

"She made you?" he asked as he sat down. "You're a little old for that, aren't you? What do you mean she *made* you?"

"She can get pretty stubborn sometimes."

"That's for sure," he said, "she sure can."

That made me mad, but I kept my mouth shut.

He puffed away for a few moments. "Look," he tried again, "why can't we make this a nice trip? Have some fun. Get to know each other."

"If you wanted to get to know me maybe you

shouldn't have taken off when I was a kid."

Even in the fading light I could see his face redden. He looked away, as if there was something in the trees that suddenly caught his attention, and stayed like that awhile. Then he nodded. When he started talking again his voice shook, and he kept his eyes on the darkened trees.

"I guess this was a bad idea, this trip. I . . . maybe I didn't think it through good enough. You're right." He turned and faced me. "It was a bad idea. Tomorrow we'll get to the Soo. There's someplace I want to take you, if it's okay with you. It won't take long. Then I'll get you a bus ticket to Thunder Bay."

He stood up and walked slowly, as if he was carrying something heavy, to the back of the van. I heard the rear door open and then slam shut. When he came back to the fire there was a bottle of whiskey in his hand.

The old man stopped beside me. I looked up at him, but he kept his face averted. His voice was quiet and trembled even more than before.

"Just for the record, Steve, there's somethin' you ought to know. I suffered too."

Slowly, holding the bottle by the neck, he walked into the trees, along the path that led to the pond.

I closed my book and looked into the fire. In *Shogun*, somebody, one of the Japanese, explained to Blackthorne how the Japanese handled their problems. He said that they put the problem "in a box" in their mind and didn't think about it for a while. When the time seemed right they got out the box and took out the problem, looked it over, then put it away again if no solution suggested itself.

I tried clearing my mind the way some of the characters in the novel seemed able to do. No way. My thoughts zapped around like pinballs in a speeded-up game, lighting up posts, buzzing and ringing. The higher the score got, the tighter I felt.

So he had suffered too. Then why did he abandon me like one of his empty beer cans? Why did he stay away? Why did he come back?

I went into the van, closing the slider behind me because a damp chilly breeze had sprung up. I clicked on the little light above the sink so the old man could see when he got back from the pond, then climbed up to my bed.

I lay there for a long time, listening to the waterfall and the wind moaning out of the night sky.

REPLAY

I decided to take a run after the final wrestling practice of the school year. Leonard had pushed me hard, knowing I'd have no formal practice again before the tournament in Thunder Bay, and I was tired and stiff. I took a long slow jog, enjoying the warm sun and the fragrant early summer breeze as I loped through the streets.

When I got back to the school I saw a bunch of the other wrestlers turning onto Birmingham Street, walking with their heads together as if they were sharing a secret. I yelled to them but they didn't hear me. Too tired to catch up with them, I entered the school.

The large L-shaped locker room was almost dark and the odour of sweat hung like smoke in the damp air. From around the corner at the far end of the room a shower hissed. As I groped my way down the main part of the room and around the corner of the L, a strange sound gradually separated itself from the hiss and gurgle of the shower. Somebody was crying. I felt along the wall for the switch. The fluorescent tubes flickered and buzzed, flooding the room with hard white light.

In the corner, behind an overturned bench, a kid lay facing the wall, curled up like a foetus. He was wearing a black singlet.

Only one wrestler on our team had a black singlet. GO ANIMAL was stencilled across the front.

"Hawk!" I cried, rushing over to him.

My first thought was that the other guys had ganged up on him. But nobody I knew would want to hurt Hawk. And nobody I knew would have had the guts to try.

He didn't respond at first, just pulled his knees up closer to his chest. Bits of paper littered the floor around him and speckled his singlet. More bits were stuck in his hair.

I threw the bench aside and grabbed his arm. "Hawk! Hawk, what's going on?"

He flinched and pulled away. "No more!" he whined. His eyes were screwed shut, like a little kid at a horror movie. I couldn't believe what I saw and heard. This was no little kid. This was almost seventy kilos of bone and muscle. This was the guy who turned into an electrified devil whenever he was in a fight.

"It's Wick," I shouted, scared by the stranger cowering in front of me. "Come on! Quit fooling around!"

I seized him again, roughly, and hauled him into

a sitting position. His chin was jammed to his chest, his arms covered his head, and he was sobbing so hard the words seemed to be jerked from his body.

"I'm . . . o-okay . . . Go on home now, Wick. I'll be all right. I'll . . . catch you later."

"Hawk, stop crying," I tried again, calmer now. "Look at me. Open your eyes. Who did this to you?" I asked, not even knowing what the "this" was. By the looks of him he hadn't been fighting. There were no scrapes or bruises, no blood.

"What the hell is this stuff, anyway?" I asked, picking up a few bits of the stiff paper. They looked like pieces torn from photographs.

Hawk was still hiding his face in his arms. "They . . . they found them," he sobbed in a voice that wasn't his. "They found them. Damn it! Why didn't I leave them at home?"

"Leave what at home? What are you talking about? What's wrong?" I shook him, trying to pry his arms away from his head, to make him look at me, but he was too strong.

"Wick, you're the only friend I have," he said desperately. "The only one left. Oh god, it's gonna be all over the school!"

I sat back on the wooden bench and leaned forward on my knees. I took a deep breath. Go easy, I said to myself. "Look, Hawk, I don't have a clue what you're talking about. So listen, try to calm down, okay? Take your time and tell me what's the matter."

He still wouldn't look at me, but his voice had a little more control when he whispered, "The guys found these . . . sex pictures."

I was relieved in a way, thinking, is this all it is? Hawk is ashamed he's human like the rest of us? I began to feel a little better, as if the universe was heading toward normal. I remembered how Hawk would never join the locker room sex talk, the bragging about girls, the constant trading of insults that the other guys kept up, calling each other fag every few seconds. I also remembered that I was always in on it, telling lies and acting big. "You talk about women as if they were meat," Hawk had said many times, so many that the guys thought he was some kind of sour-faced puritan.

I brushed some of the paper bits from his shoulder. "Relax, Hawk. Lots of the guys have pictures. Every guy I know likes pictures of naked women. It's natural. It's no big deal."

"They were pictures," came a voice so choked with sobbing that I could barely make it out, "of guys."

"What? I thought you said *guys.*" This was really getting crazy.

He took his arms away from his face, but he still wouldn't look up. "They were pictures of men."

"Let me get this straight. You're telling me that you had some sex pictures of men."

He nodded.

"So . . . " My mind began to race over strange ground, the way it does when you're in unknown territory and you're trying to find a landmark to get your bearings. "So they said . . . so they razzed you and said 'Hawk's a fag,' right? Is that why you're so upset?"

At last he raised his head and looked at me, straight into my eyes, his own eyes so full of fear they seemed to vibrate with energy. I had never seen his face like that—terrified, wounded, beaten.

"Wick," he said thickly, "I *am* gay."

It was like a full-out punch to my solar plexus. I couldn't breathe. A sick burning fear rushed in where my breath had been. I slowly rose from the bench.

"Yeah, right. Very funny, Hawk. You're a panic."

But it wasn't funny. The tears streaming from his eyes and the sobs wracking his body told me more than his words could do.

I stepped back.

"Wick, please, *please!*"

Blindly I moved away from him, grabbed my gym bag, tore my clothes from the hook on the wall, backing away as if he was a leper and if I touched him or even breathed the same air I'd be contaminated. I turned and ran.

The wail of pain chased me through the locker room, slamming off the walls, echoing inside my skull. "Wick!" he screamed. "Wick, please!"

SIXTEEN

THE ECHO BECAME THE ROAR of wind punctuated by a low uneven booming, like the irregular heartbeat of a huge beast. I jerked upright, suddenly awake.

Rain pounded on the roof of the van. The canvas sides of the pop top boomed as they flexed and snapped with each powerful gust of the wind.

I climbed down from the bed and knuckled the sleep from my eyes. It was still dark outside. I looked at my watch. Two a.m.

The old man wasn't there. His bed wasn't pulled out.

I drew on my clothes and rummaged around for a flashlight, finding one under the driver's seat. When I yanked open the side door the wind gushed in, bringing rain. I jumped out and quickly pulled the door closed. Within seconds I was soaked to the skin. I swept the campsite with the light, saw the two overturned lawn chairs, the dead wet ashes of the fire, the hatchet stuck in a log.

The weak yellow light-beam bounced ahead of me as I made my way through the tossing evergreens down to the water. Whipped by the rainy wind, I played the light back and forth along the shore until the faint yellow circle found him. He was lying half under the boughs of an evergreen on the edge of the bush, legs drawn up to his chest, arms crossed, one hand clutching the almost empty bottle. Tears of rain coursed in tiny rivulets across his face. I pulled the bottle out of his grip and tossed it aside.

"Hey, wake up."

He groaned as I dragged him to a sitting position. Great, I thought. I managed to haul him to his feet and picked him up in a fireman's carry and slowly worked my way back along the path to the van. He wasn't very heavy.

Inside, I lowered the old man to the floor. I set up his bed, then lifted him under the arms and turned him so he could sit on the edge. He fell backwards, sprawled on the bed. I hauled him upright again. His eyes opened as I tried to pull his sopping bush shirt off.

"Whozat?" he mumbled.

"It's me. Hold still." I got the bush shirt and T-shirt off and started working on his boots.

"She stole him off me," he mumbled.

When I had done with his boots and socks I stood up. He was crying.

"She took my little boy. My little Stevie. I hadda leave or she'd tell everybody."

I lowered him to his back. His bare wet chest heaved as I pulled off his soaking wet jeans and underwear. With a dish towel I dried him as well as I could, then pulled his sleeping bag onto him like a giant sock.

I stripped off my own clothes, letting them fall to the floor and leaving them as I wiped myself off with the towel. I snapped off the light above the sink and climbed up into my bed.

What had he meant when he said she'd tell everybody? The "she" was probably my mother. Had she kicked him out because he was a drinker? Had my father done something that made her force him to leave? Why would she do that to me?

I heard him whimpering in his sleep while deep in the cellar of my memory the laser jumped frantically from postcard to postcard, sending powerful messages surging along the cable and flashing like lighting into my mind.

I lay awake for hours, the old man moaning in his sleep beneath me while the wind cried around us.

SEVENTEEN

THE NEXT MORNING, as the grey light of dawn leaked into the wet world outside the van, I put the coffee on and dressed in dry clothes. I was tired and raw and depressed—and it was only Wednesday. I'd been with the old man since Sunday, but it seemed more like three weeks than three days.

I stepped outside and headed to the washroom down the road. The wind had lessened but it was still there, pushing grey clouds across a sullen sky. The bush was water-logged and quiet and the mosquitoes were out in force. I got back into the van and turned off the stove, then woke the old man up. When he looked like he could sit up without help I poured out a coffee and handed it to him.

He sat on the edge of the bed, his sleeping bag gathered around his lower body, noisily sipping, saying nothing. He looked pale, his eyes bloodshot, his hair spiky, his stubble dark against his skin.

"Think you could drive this thing?" he said finally. His hand shook as he raised the cup of steaming coffee to his mouth.

"I've never driven a standard, but I could try, I guess."

"Try," he urged. "I'm in no shape to drive. When you get out to the highway, that's Highway 17, turn right. You'll get to the outskirts of the Soo in a couple of hours. Wake me up then and I'll drive us into town to Sharon's."

I didn't ask who Sharon was. He put the empty cup down, slumped back on the bed and curled up, gathering the bag around him. He was asleep in an instant.

I put the wet lawn chairs in the back, gathered up the hatchet and the supper dishes, and pulled down the pop top, clicking the latches into place. The key was in the ignition. I started the van and fiddled with the knobs on the dash to get some heat going to drive away the dampness.

I stalled half a dozen times just backing out of the campsite, jerking the van back and forth like a demented rocking horse. Luckily the old man was dead to the world or I'd have rattled his brains permanently.

Once out on the road, I cranked the wheel, shoved down hard on the clutch pedal and tried to find first gear. The van shuddered and bucked but it moved in the right direction. I jammed it into second gear and left it there, steering carefully, not bothering to stop at the park gate for fear I'd look like an idiot trying to get going again. I had to come to a halt when I reached Highway 17, though. I waited until there wasn't another vehicle in sight before I jerked and sputtered my way onto the pavement, crawling along like a bug as I slowly worked my way through the gears.

After a little while I began to relax. I turned on the radio and classical music boomed out of the speakers.

After a couple of shots at the seek button I found a rock station and settled back for the drive.

The highway turned and dipped, coiled around hills and climbed over the ones it couldn't avoid. It crossed rivers, went through small towns and Indian reserves. I began to enjoy the drive, and as I rolled along I did a little planning.

I figured I'd take the old man at his word and take the bus the rest of the way to Thunder Bay. No matter how I looked at it, this trip wasn't working out. At all.

It was still a moody overcast day when I saw the signs saying we were almost to Sault Ste. Marie, or the Soo as everybody calls it. I was driving along flat land, farms on my right stretching away to the mountains, the blue waters of Georgian Bay on my left. When the road widened to four lanes, signs promising junk-food joints appeared and I knew we were close. I pulled off at a picnic spot. I forgot to put in the clutch and when the van was almost stopped it bucked a few times before it shuddered to a halt. The engine died. I turned off the ignition and got out.

I visited the outdoor toilet, then woke up the old man. It was like trying to push King Kong back up to the top of the Empire State Building. He groaned and rolled out of my reach, promised to get up, then flopped back and closed his eyes. Finally I turned the radio on and cranked up the volume. A Rush tune boomed out of the speakers loud enough to rip the top off the van. That did it.

Once he was up, the old man was quiet and sheepish. He got himself dressed and slid behind the wheel.

We drove into the Soo, passing shopping malls and motels on Wellington Street, then the old man wended his way through a residential neighbourhood. He pulled into a gravel drive in front of a small frame bungalow and parked beside a rusted-out Honda Civic.

I got out and looked around. The house reminded me of our old bunaglow on 23rd Street—the one I grew up in. It was white, trimmed in dark green, with shrubs along the front under the windows on either side of the door. From out back came the wail of country-western music. I followed the old man around the side of the house.

There was a shed there, with stove wood piled high along one side. A woman raised an axe high above her and brought it down on the birch log that stood atop a splitting block. *Whack!* The log split neatly in two and the halves wobbled briefly before toppling to the ground.

"You never were any good at that," the old man said.

The woman turned and her face lit up. "Jack!" she exclaimed. "You're here!"

She leaned the axe against the chopping block, shut off a beat-up portable radio at her feet and walked quickly toward us. She and the old man wrapped themselves up in a big hug, kissed, and both talked at once for a second.

She finally seemed to notice me. "You must be Steve," she said, smiling. "Welcome to the Soo."

I had to hand it to the old man. She was pretty good-looking, with long black hair caught behind with an elastic band, big dark eyes and a great bod. She wore faded jeans, running shoes split along the soles and a checkered bush shirt with the sleeves rolled up, showing tanned forearms.

"Hi," I managed as we shook hands. Her hands were strong and rough.

Sharon turned back to the old man. "You look a little the worse for wear," she commented, and the old man gave her a guilty look. "How about some tea?"

"Sounds great."

She led us through the back door into a small kitchen. The old man and I sat down at a painted wooden table while Sharon put the kettle on and got the tea ready.

"You like tea, Steve?" she asked over her shoulder.

"Call me Wick, please. Yeah, tea's fine."

She turned. "What did you—"

"It's his nickname," the old man explained. "He likes it better than his real name."

Sharon smiled, melting away my resentment at the old man for speaking for me. "Well, sometime you'll have to tell me where you picked up a handle like that. Anyway," she said to the old man, "I've missed you."

"Me too."

I got the impression that if I hadn't been there they'd have been in the sack instead of going on about how long it had been since they'd seen each other. Luckily, the whistling kettle interrupted this fascinating conversation.

Sharon brought the cups, tea pot, milk and sugar to the table and sat down beside the old man.

"Your show—" she began.

The old man held up his hand. "Sorry, Sharon, can we talk about that later?"

"Sure. Yeah." She sipped her tea, frowning.

"What show?" I asked Sharon.

The old man frowned. "Nothin'."

We made small talk while we sipped our tea, then the old man asked if anybody minded if he had a snooze. Nobody minded—as if we were going to say anything—so he left the kitchen.

"What's happening, Sharon? What's this about a show?"

"You any good at chopping wood, Wick?" Sharon asked.

I knew she didn't want to say anything more. "Oh, I guess I could manage." Which was a lie. I had never chopped wood in my life. We didn't have too much call for chopping in a condo in Etobicoke.

Sharon took me out back and stood there watching while I fumbled around, pretending I knew what I was doing. After all, I thought, how hard can it be if she can do it? Well, it wasn't hard, but there were a few tricks to make it easy, like using the splitting axe's weight instead of driving it down with full force and burying the head in the chopping block and sending the pieces of wood rocketing away on either side like they were shot from a cannon. Like using a wedge on the logs that had big knot holes in them.

The thing was, Sharon explained it in a way that didn't make me feel like a loser. She went back into the house and left me to the job.

I kept at it for quite a while. It felt good to use my muscles again after a few days doing nothing. It felt even better to be hitting something. I was hot and sweating and I felt loose, like I could go all day. But

Sharon called me in for supper, thanked me for my help, and put a steaming plate of spaghetti in front of me.

The old man didn't join us. We ate in silence, concentrating on the food while cowboy music moaned and complained from the radio on the windowsill. As we did the dishes Sharon told me she worked in the maintenance section of the steel plant in town. She had been laid off a week ago, temporarily, she hoped. Then she asked me about school and my wrestling and all that stuff. I told her about how I got my name, about the upcoming tournament. I liked being with her, to tell the truth. She was one attractive woman. Maybe the old man isn't such a wimp after all, I thought.

We watched TV for a while and I went to bed early. Sharon made up the couch for me in the living room and I fell asleep almost as soon as my head hit the pillow.

EIGHTEEN

THE NEXT MORNING I WOKE UP to the howl of opera music. Oh god, not her too, I thought. I pulled on my jeans and T-shirt and walked barefoot into the kitchen. Sharon was sitting at the table, spooning something that looked like oatmeal into her mouth. She was wearing a white dress and her hair was woven in a French braid.

"Okay if I have a shower?" I asked.

"Good morning. Sure, help yourself. I hope Jack left some dry towels." When I turned toward the bathroom she added, "By the way, we're going out after you eat. Jack wants me to take you somewhere."

"Oh? Where?"

"I'm not supposed to say."

"Why not? What's the big mystery?"

"Well, if I told you it wouldn't be a surprise." She smiled.

I just shrugged my shoulders and headed for the bathroom. About half an hour later we went out to her car. It was about ten o'clock and the sun blazed out of a hard blue sky. The Civic's interior was like a torture chamber and the black plastic-covered seats fried us.

When Sharon fired up the car it sounded worse than the old man's van. We wound down the windows—mine would only go halfway—and took off, me wishing

98

we were in my mother's BMW with its air conditioning.

Sharon drove down near the waterfront, bumped across some railroad tracks and parked in the lot of a huge mall beside an old building that looked like a train station. She pointed across the lot to a newer building that had a huge sign depicting a polar bear. "That's where you can take the train to the Agawa Canyon," she said.

"Oh, yeah, the old man mentioned he wanted to take me on that trip. He said the scenery was great."

She looked at me sharply. "Why do you call him that?"

"What?"

"The old man."

I felt my face flush. "I don't know. I just do."

"Come on, we can get in the back way. We don't need a ticket."

"A ticket for what?"

But she had already headed around the back of the building. She opened a narrow wooden door and led the way in. We went down a darkened hall into a large room flooded with sunlight from the north windows. The room was carpeted and dotted with pedestals of different heights, cut from peeled logs varnished to a dull gold. On top of each pedestal was an animal carved from wood—bears, squirrels, different kinds of birds, including a couple of wicked-looking hawks.

At the far end of the room was a large wooden desk. A woman sat behind it, a phone tucked between shoulder and neck. The old man was perched on the edge of the desk, talking to another man standing beside him, holding his unlit pipe in one hand, his thumb slowly moving back and forth on the bowl. The old man was dressed up—for him. He had on a crisp white short-sleeved shirt, clean narrow-wale cords and moccasins.

"Why don't you take a look around," Sharon said, her voice still a little frosty. "I'll see what Jack's up to."

Art doesn't really ring my chimes all that much, but even I could tell those sculptures were good. Really good. The animals were carved with careful detail, the wood glowed, the soft curves of the grain added life and energy. Especially the hawks. They were fierce, with sharp curved beaks, glaring eyes, aggressive talons reaching for their prey. But they were beautiful too, kind of noble.

While I looked, moving slowly from pedestal to pedestal, something was niggling at the back of my mind. On the pedestal beside each sculpture was a small white card with the name of the piece—"Hawk in Flight," "Leaping Trout," stuff like that—along with a date. A lot of the cards had red dots stuck on them.

I looked over at the old man. He was watching me. He had a strange look on his face, like he was expecting something. Then it hit me. The niggling at the back of my mind.

This was the big surprise.

These sculptures were his.

Random images flashed into my mind like strobe lights. Curls of cedar wood on the floor of the van. The empty work bench in the cellar of the house that told me when I was seven that the old man had left. The missing box of carving tools. The cedar shaving in the cold empty apartment on rue Mont Carmel.

I turned my back on him, pretending to examine a carving. "Native mask" it was called. A gruesome, grimacing face showing primitive fear and confusion.

I felt a lump in my throat and a hot glow in my chest. The old man had tricked me into coming here. I was supposed to be proud of him and his big show-and-not-tell. "Look at us," the sculptures seemed to say, "aren't we great?"

I wanted to get out of there. I moved slowly toward the front entrance, but to get there I had to pass a big easel just inside the double glass doors. There was a sign on the easel: "Jack Chandler Collection". Beside it was a sculpture on a plaster pedestal, situated so everyone coming into the gallery had to pass by it. I stepped up to it, pretending to be interested, so I could get to the door without Sharon or the old man noticing.

One look at the sculpture and I froze. This one wasn't a fish or bird or animal. It was larger than the others, so big you'd need two hands to lift it, and it showed something I knew about. Two men wrestling. The man being thrown was caught in mid-flight. The thrower had him in an underhook, arching his back in a perfect curve, legs bent at the knee, every muscle on his body hard and tight, bulging with the strain of lifting the helpless opponent into the air.

A perfect *Supplé*.

It was exactly like the *Toronto Star* photo hanging on my bedroom wall. Only better.

The card on the pedestal read, "Father's Pride (Not For Sale)".

Almost unconsciously I reached out and ran my fingers along the smooth glowing wood, my hand shaking. I turned and bolted through the glass doors, almost knocking down an old woman on her way in, and ran across the sunny parking lot toward the wide doors that led into the mall.

REPLAY

I was hunkered down at the edge of the mat, eyeing my opponent on the other side. He was doing knee bends, looking loose, confident. I wished I felt that way. My stomach was in a knot. My limbs tingled weakly. I stood and pulled off my sweats. The ref would be calling us to the centre of the mat any second now.

"Give him hell, Wick," Leonard growled. I could hardly hear him over the roar of the crowd.

"Won't be easy," I said. "This guy Park has never been thrown or pinned."

"What? Where did you hear that? What are you talking about, never been thrown?"

"It's true, sir. I overheard a couple of his teammates talking a while ago."

Leonard laughed. "Hey, Wick, get with the program! That's the oldest trick in the book. Those guys threw a psych on you. You're not going to fall for that, are you?"

The ref's whistle shrilled. He called out our names.

"I've *seen* this guy thrown," Leonard added. "More than once. He isn't even in your league."

I felt my confidence rushing back like a fast tide as I stepped to the centre of the mat and shook hands with Park.

After what seemed an eternity the ref held my arm in the air. Aching all over and breathing hard, I went to my opponent's corner to shake hands with his coach.

"Nice work, Chandler," he said. "You did what nobody's done." I must have looked confused because he added, "Jason's never been pinned. That *Supplé* was magnificent."

NINETEEN

ONCE INSIDE THE MALL, I stopped, not sure what to do next, not sure what I was doing there in the first place.

It was cool and dim inside after the heat and glare of the parking lot. I walked among the shoppers, trying to get my bearings, to make some sense of everything. Once, in a wrestling match, when I was a brand-new cadet, I got thrown. I landed so hard it knocked the wind—and the sense—out of me. When I got up I was so dazed I didn't realize the match was over. That was how I felt as I wandered past the hardware stores, clothing shops, candy and ice-cream stands. I felt tricked but I knew I hadn't been. I was choked up by the sculpture of me that the old man had carved—who knew how long it had taken him?—but still angry with him. Mostly I felt confused.

When I thought more about the sculptures I realized how good the old man was. You didn't have to be an artsy-fartsy type—which I wasn't—to see that he had tremendous talent. The sculptures were so real, but not like a perfect drawing that has no feeling to it. Those carvings were full of life, as if the person who did them had some kind of deep understanding. And the one of me, well, it showed all the things that I liked about wrestling—power, strength, agility . . . I don't know, the honourableness of two guys going at each other, but with respect, in the oldest sport known to man. How had the old man done it? I thought. How had he *known* that?

Another damn mystery.

The mall's corridor ended at a huge food store. I shoved a stray shopping cart out of my way and turned to walk back the way I had come. The big question, I realized, was even bigger now. He knew about me, knew about the photo that was framed on my wall, knew how much wrestling meant to me. And yet he was never around, not like other divorced parents who saw their kids regularly, went to their music recitals or football games and made sure they were around at Christmas. The ones kids called Sunday parents.

Then I realized my attitude toward him had never really changed since I was seven. I was proud of him and hated him at the same time.

I didn't want it all dragged up again. But I wanted to know *why*. That was what tortured me.

Sharon was waiting at the main doors of the mall.

"You okay?" she asked. Her face was calm but her eyes were anxious.

"Yeah, sure. Never been better."

She ignored the sarcasm. "Come on, I'll drive you home."

As we pulled out of the parking lot in that little hot-box of a car, Sharon said above the racket of the muffler, "Wick, mind if I ask a favour?"

I had been staring at my hands as they twisted in my lap. I looked at her. She was watching the road.

"What?"

"Did you know," she began haltingly, "did you

know your dad has a drinking problem?"

"I figured." You didn't have to be a genius.

"Well, I don't know how to say this. I mean, I'm not telling you how to act or anything, but if you could try to get along with him it would help."

"Oh, so it's my fault."

Sharon turned onto her street and shifted up through the gears. "No, Wick, I'm not saying that. Of course it isn't. But it's *about* you. And if he felt . . . well, better about you and him, it might help him lay off the booze."

"How could it be about me? I haven't seen him or heard from him for ten years."

Sharon turned into her driveway. The car bumped to a stop beside the old man's van. She looked at me for a moment.

"Maybe you never realized—you were what, seven or eight?—but leaving home almost destroyed your father. That's what got him drinking."

"Yeah, then why did he go? Why didn't he come back?"

Sharon sighed. "He'll have to tell you that himself."

"He hasn't told me bugger-all, Sharon. Nobody has. And you know what? I'm sick of it, sick of mysteries. Nobody wants to tell me anything. Are you the reason he left?"

"No, Wick. I met your father five years ago. It wasn't about another woman, I can tell you that much."

"And what the hell was today supposed to prove? Well, it didn't prove anything, you know that? So he's a great artist. So what?" I slammed the dash with the flat of my hand, making Sharon jump. "Today just made things *worse!*"

Suddenly it was dead quiet inside the Honda. Sharon stared ahead at the woodpile, gripping the steering wheel, her knuckles white with the strain.

She tipped her head a little. "See that van?"

"Yeah, so?"

"Almost everything your father owns is in there."

"So?" I said again, right away feeling bad that I'd snapped at her. None of this was her fault, I knew. She was caught in the middle.

Sharon looked right into my eyes. "His keys are on the dresser in my bedroom. If he finds out I helped you," she added, "he'll leave me. I know he will."

I got out of the Honda. I bent over, leaning on the roof, and looked at her. Her hands still clutched the wheel as if she were hanging on for her life.

"You love him, don't you?" I said.

She sobbed and reached for the key. The engine roared to life. I stepped back and shut the door. I watched her back out of the driveway and pull away down the street. Why would someone like *her* love *him?* I wondered. I went into the house.

TWENTY

I KNEW WHAT SHARON HAD INVITED me to do and I knew I was going to do it. In her bedroom sunlight washed over the cheap furniture and the faded blue counterpane on the bed. One of the old man's shirts hung from the doorknob. I found his keys on the dresser, just as Sharon had said.

I opened the van's rear door first because that's where he kept all his stuff. As I searched I lifted the canvas bags and cartons down and placed them carefully on the gravel so I could put each one back in exactly the same place. I didn't really give a damn if he found out I was snooping around, but I had to think about Sharon.

The first carton was small. It contained a couple of decks of cards, a cribbage board and four old shoeboxes. One shoebox was full of tapes, lined up neatly, so that the backs of the cases were upright. In the centre of each, partially covering the label, was a red dot, the kind you can buy in office supply stores. All the tapes were Mozart. That figures, I thought, he's a classical music nut. What didn't figure was the neatness.

I put the lid back on and examined another shoebox. Same thing, but this time the dots were blue, and the tapes were Puccini operas. The third box was yellow dots on country-and-western classics tapes. The last shoebox contained ten or eleven CDS, with all the colours represented, along with green dots for operas.

I replaced the shoeboxes in the carton and set it aside. The next was full of cold-weather clothing. I groped around among the sweaters, mitts and stuff, finding nothing of interest.

The third carton was heavy. It contained blocks of cedar and pine. For his carving, I figured. I set that box down in the driveway with the others. Next came a metal tool box with a hinged lid that opened to reveal wrenches, pliers, screwdrivers, a tube of body-filler and a couple of whetstones. So far I hadn't found anything earth-shaking.

The last cardboard carton was the smallest. I lifted it down to the ground and knelt beside it, then pried open the interlocked flaps. There was what looked like a ratty old shirt rolled into a ball, but when I took hold of it I realized something was wrapped up in it. I unrolled it carefully to reveal a china bowl, a small silver cup and a silver spoon. The bowl tugged at my memory. Around the edge were rabbits, the kind you see in kids' books, running on their back legs, holding each other's paws so they formed a chain of running bunnies around the rim of the bowl. The bunnies were from those Beatrix Potter books the old man would buy me but never read to me. "Ask your mother," he'd say. But she never had the time. I examined the bowl more carefully.

It was my bowl. It was the one I had used as a baby.

The cup had my name engraved in graceful flowing letters: *Steven Chandler*, along with my birthdate. The spoon was one of those baby spoons with the handle looped back on itself. It had my name on it too.

I stared at the objects, seeing quick Replays of myself in a high chair. My hands shook as I carefully rolled up the bowl, cup and spoon in the shirt.

I removed a big scrapbook from the box and set it aside. At the bottom of the box were three rubber stamps, and an old stamp pad. I knew that one stamp would say DAD, another would show the address of the bungalow I grew up in, the newer one, the address of the condo. But I looked at them anyway, at the raised rubber numbers and letters.

Taking a deep breath, I picked up the scrapbook. The first few pages held pictures of me as a baby and as a little kid. The photos were glued to the black background. One or two showed me and the old man. There were no labels, no dates and no pictures of my mother. The next page held a copy of the program from my graduation from 20th Street School. Then came a few pages of photos from the local newspaper showing me at various wrestling meets. In one of them Hawk and I stood with our arms around each other's shoulders, grinning like fools.

As I had expected by that point, I found the photo that the old man used to do the carving of me, identical to the one that I had framed and hanging on my wall. This one was ragged, as if it had been handled a lot. I looked closer. There were faint pencil lines drawn with a straight-edge and protractor to note the angles of the two figures.

I didn't need to see any more. I put all these things carefully into the carton and replaced all the cartons and bags in the back of the van exactly as I had found them. I locked up the van and went to the chopping block in the yard. I started whaling away with the axe, harder than Sharon had showed me, harder than I had to.

"You bastard," I said as I slammed the axe into the wood. "You stupid bastard."

This time I was talking about myself.

TWENTY-ONE

SHARON AND THE OLD MAN came back about supper time. I was at the kitchen table having a cup of tea, nursing the blisters on my hands, and there was an awesome pile of stove wood out in the yard. The old man had had a few. He came in, took a look at me, went to the fridge to get a beer, then left the kitchen. I heard the bedroom door slam.

Sharon asked me if I was hungry. When I shook my head she went to the bedroom too. The door slammed again. I heard them talking—not arguing, but talking seriously. It went on for a while, then I heard Sharon's voice, louder than before.

"Why don't you just tell him? He'll understand."

"No!" the old man shouted.

Right after that he came out of the room and into the kitchen, patting his pockets. "You seen my keys?" he asked.

A hot sinking feeling rushed into my gut as I suddenly felt the bunch of keys pressing against my leg in the pocket of my jeans. I looked up at the old man as he searched the kitchen counter. Frantically I tried to think of something.

"Uh, why don't you sit down for a minute."

"Huh? Why?" The old man looked at me like I had a flower growing out of my forehead.

"I'd, um, I'd like to talk to you about the show. Here, let me get you another . . . um, a beer."

I went to the fridge, hoping there'd be another beer left. I should have known. There were more than half a dozen. I twisted the top off one.

"Sit down," I said, "and relax."

The old man was still looking at me strangely. No wonder, I thought guiltily. This is the first time I've talked normally to him since he picked me up in Toronto. He sat down and took a pull on the beer.

I heard the bedroom door open but Sharon didn't appear.

"Anyway, like I said, I really liked the show. It was—"

"So how come you took off?"

Good question, I thought. "I don't know. When I saw the sculpture by the door I was sort of shocked, I guess."

The old man considered this. He set the bottle down on the table. "Well, guess I can't blame you."

At that point Sharon came in and said brightly, "Anybody want coffee?" which was a pretty lame question, since I had half a cup of tea left and the old man had most of his beer. She started fussing around with the coffee makings anyway.

The old man suddenly found his beer bottle interesting. He stared at it and started to run his thumbnail through the label, top to bottom.

"Where did you get the picture of me wrestling?" I asked. "The one you used for the sculpture."

Sharon shot me a worried look. I realized too late what I had given away.

"I mean," I added hastily, "I assume you worked from a photo. The sculpture was so life-like."

But the old man didn't seem to notice. "Sharon saved it for me. She has a friend in T.O. who looks out for stuff about you in the paper."

He continued to pick fiercely at the label on the bottle. He looked up at Sharon, then back to the label. "I did it for you," he said. "I wanted to make up for . . . all those years, even though I knew I couldn't."

I felt my throat thicken. I glanced at Sharon, who had given up the show of making coffee. She stood leaning against the sink, arms crossed. She nodded to me.

I looked back at the old man, feeling my face suddenly hot. "Will you tell me one thing?" I blurted. "Why did you leave? How could you do that to me?"

"I had to," he said.

"*Why?* What do you mean?"

"She made me." He said it so softly I could hardly hear. But I remembered our argument a few days before at Chutes Park. He'd said I didn't have to come. I had told him Mom made me and he had said I was too old to be told what to do.

All the hurt and anger began to rush in again, the way the wind rushes into your house when you open the door on a stormy night, and I started to get mad.

"Couldn't you at least have told me *why?*"

"No."

"Bullshit!" I cried. "You could've. You didn't even say goodbye when you left, didn't say hello in a letter. You just sent those stupid postcards. You were so damn lazy you didn't even write out the address! Don't tell me you loved me and you're sorry and you missed me. Save that crap, will you."

"I—"

"Jack," Sharon said in a calm voice, "*tell* him!"

The old man was facing me finally, his face wracked with pain and something worse than pain that I couldn't identify.

"Steve, I . . . I just couldn't," he said. "I—"

"Yeah, you *couldn't*. Sure. Couldn't drop a line to your own son. What are you, for god's sake, illiterate or—"

At that instant I knew what I saw in his face along with the pain. It was humiliation. And at that instant things dropped into place the way the tumblers drop into place when you put the right key in a lock and turn it. Things from way back in the past. Things from the present.

The old man used to listen to the news and talk back to the radio every morning while we had breakfast. But he never read the paper.

He bought me dozens of books, but never read them to me.

He would never help me with my homework, but he'd spend hours helping me with a Lego construction.

When we were shopping in Sudbury he drove into the wrong place—the I.D.A. drugstore instead of the IGA grocery. When he asked directions to the IGA, he asked for landmarks, not street names.

His tapes and CDs were arranged by coloured dots. He sent postcards with my address and DAD stamped on them. No handwriting. No signature.

I felt like a fire cracker had exploded in my brain.

"Jesus," I said as his face reddened. "Jesus, you *couldn't* write to me! You . . . " I ran out of words.

"Go ahead and say it!" he shouted, throwing his pipe clattering onto the table. "Go ahead! I'm illiterate! Your father's a stupid moron!"

"That's not what I—"

He jumped up, kicking back his chair, and turned to the door. But Sharon was on him in a flash. "No, no! Not this time, Jack! This time you *don't* leave!" But she couldn't hold him back. He stumbled out the door, letting it slap shut behind him.

Thoughts whirled inside my head the way dust swirls in the corner of a building on a windy day.

"You knew, didn't you?" I said to Sharon.

She nodded. "Thank god it's finally out," she said, the way you say 'Oh boy' when you put down a heavy load. "I couldn't tell you, Wick. I'm sorry, but I owed it to him to keep my mouth shut. I promised him. Now you've got to go out there and tell him to stay."

I was too mixed up to think for myself so I did as she said. I ran outside and found the old man yanking at the van door, cursing, as if yelling at it would unlock it. I stood for a moment, wracking my brains, not knowing what to say to him.

I reached into my pocket and held out his keys to him in my open palm. He looked at me, his face streaked with tears and humiliation, then down at the keys.

"You can go if you want," I said. "I don't know if I can ever forgive you for leaving the first time. That's the honest truth. But now I'm asking you to stay."

He took the keys from my outstretched hand, then weighed them in his own hand, as he looked first at the house, then at the van, then at me.

He put the keys into his pocket and went back into the house. I followed him in.

TWENTY-TWO

"TO EXPLAIN ALL THIS I GOT TO GO back a ways," the old man said around the stem of his pipe.

The three of us were sitting at the table. We had eaten supper and Sharon and the old man had done the dishes while I stacked the mountain of firewood I had chopped that afternoon. The old man hadn't asked me how I had come up with his keys and I didn't tell him.

"Your mother and me met a little more than a year before you were born. I found the job at the tire plant and she was takin' business courses at Humber College. We went out for about six months before she took me home to see your grandparents. They didn't like me, but you probably know that. No education, no good job, no prospects for one. Sometimes I wondered myself what your mother saw in me. I knew that part of the reason she married me was to rebel against her parents, but I loved her, and when you love somebody you don't look things over too close.

"Anyway, we got married when your mother was still in college and by the time she graduated she was pregnant with you, and a few months later you were born." The old man paused, took a couple of drags on the pipe, a half smile on his lips. "You sure were a cute baby. I was in the delivery room while you were gettin' born.

118

"Well, stayin' at home and takin' care of you woke your mother up to reality real quick. That's when things started to go bad. Oh, I don't mean it was because of you, don't think that, but she grew so damned frustrated at home all day. I guess she had lots of time to think things over. And I guess she realized she made a mistake marryin' me and tyin' herself down.

"I figured it out little by little, over time. I can still remember the day I realized she didn't love me no more and maybe she never really did. But we went on. A year or so later she wanted to go to university, so we scrimped and saved and borrowed a bit here and there. She took accountin', and when you were six she graduated, got her papers and stepped right into a pretty good job. She got ahead fast—you know how smart she is. And ambitious."

He got up and poured coffee into Sharon's mug and his own.

I was wondering how Sharon was feeling about all this stuff. I mean, sitting there, listening to the old man talk about being in love with my mother and all.

"Anyhow," he went on, "the more she accomplished, the farther she got from me. Hardly spoke to me. Came home from work, had supper with us and worked on stuff she brought home from the office.

"I knew she was ashamed of me, just like her parents were. She never said nothin', of course, but I knew. We fought quite a bit, and a couple of times she said she was gonna leave, but I always talked her out of it. I said it was better for you if we stuck together, and I didn't want to lose her. But deep inside I knew it was only a matter of time."

He cleared his throat a few times and fiddled with

his pipe, tamping the tobacco down, relighting it.

"Did . . . did she know?"

He looked up at me. "No. I never told her. I was gonna, after we got married, then I was scared to."

"But how could you keep that a secret from your own wife? How come she didn't notice?"

"Oh, there's ways. She knew when she met me I never touched a book. Lots of people don't. And after a life-time of coverin' up, you learn a lot of strategies. Besides, like I said, once things started to do downhill we didn't spend much time together. We didn't talk much any more. Listen," he added, and his tone changed, "I'm not sayin' it was all her fault. I can be a real horse's ass to live with sometimes. She'll tell you that."

He nodded to Sharon, who smiled and patted his arm.

"True," she said, "but worth it."

"Anyway, time came she got her promotion. She was real happy about that, I can tell you. The bosses in the company were having a big party for all the staff and they decided to announce her promotion at the party. She said I was invited too. I tried to get out of it—what did I want, sippin' wine with a bunch of suits, not knowin' what to say to anybody—but she said if I didn't go it would look bad for her. I decided I was bein' selfish and maybe I should go. Stupidest thing I ever did.

"So there I was with all them confident educated people in some fancy lounge at the University of Toronto where one of the bosses had connections, tryin' not to put my foot in my mouth and disgrace your mother. I had a few glasses of wine to loosen up, didn't talk unless I had to. Then the shit hit the fan.

"Your mother and me were in a group of about half a dozen, talkin'—them, not me—mostly stuff about the office. Her boss was there, his wife, a younger guy from the office and his wife. The younger man was one of these loud pushy types, thinks he knows everythin'. 'Hey, Jack, I must show you this joke card one of my clients gave me,' he says. He reaches into his jacket pocket and pulls out a card about the size of a birthday card and hands it to me, smilin'. There were a couple of cartoon characters on it, a man and a woman, both naked, and the woman's got a surprised look on her face. There was some writin' underneath.

"I looked up at the guy. 'Go on, read it to us,' he says. I looked down at it like I was readin', then tried to fake it. I laughed and handed it back. Your mother's boss says to me, 'Read it to us, Jack.' He had a big grin on his face.

"I figured they were settin' me up, makin' a joke or something because I was only a factory worker, no education, and they were hot-shot intellectuals, and I got mad as hell. Who did they think they were, I thought. A bunch of puffed-up bastards in expensive suits. Your mother had a look on her face like I was embarrassin' her in front of the jerks and phonies she worked with. I got even madder when I realized that.

"'I forgot my glasses,' I says. 'I can't make it out.'"

"Your mother laughed the way you do when you're real nervous. 'Jack!' she says, 'you don't wear—'

"I cut her off real quick. 'I can't make it out. Do you hear what I'm sayin'? I *can't.*'

"Your mother turned deathly white, then red, then her mouth dropped open in shock. Because she understood, see, she realized what I was tellin' her. She excused herself and dashed off, spillin' her wine on her dress as she rushed away. I went after her and caught up with her outside. That was some trip back home, I'll tell you."

The old man related the story as calmly as he could, but his hands shook like leaves on a branch when he relit his pipe.

"A couple of days later she comes home from the office real late—you were in bed—and says she wants to talk. She thought things through, she says. The marriage is over, it's been over for a long time, and now she wants to call it quits. One of us has to leave, she says, and it isn't gonna be her. So she wants me to get out. She says if I don't she'll tell you I'm illiterate, she'll phone the factory and tell them. She'll tell everybody she can. But if I agree to leave she won't tell nobody. Solemn promise. She says she's gonna get a divorce from me anyway, and she's gonna fight for custody of you if she has to. And if I fight her, she'll bring it all out in court that I can't read or write, and she'll win. No judge is gonna give custody to an illiterate father who can hardly hold a job instead of an educated mother who just got a big promotion in an accountin' company. She said I had to go away and stay away."

The old man wiped his eyes with the back of his hand. Sharon got up and stood behind him and held his shoulders. He looked into his coffee, then at me.

"I'm sorry, Steve. Maybe I should have fought her. But I knew I'd lose, and I couldn't stand it if everybody knew. They'd have laughed at me. They'd've thought I was nothin'. I'd hid it for my whole life, I was so ashamed. From everybody. Even from your mother.

You meant everythin' to me. I was your hero, I knew that. How could I face my little boy, him knowin' his dad was an illiterate idiot?

"It broke my heart, leavin' you, Steve. It broke my heart."

I felt the tears come as Replays flashed into my mind and I saw myself waiting for him to come back home, ripping up the postcards, shoving my BMX off the trestle into the river. Missing him and hating him at the same time.

I looked at Sharon. She held tight to my father's shaking shoulders. Her eyes were telling me what to do. I stood up, stepped over to my father. Sharon backed away and I put my arms around him and he grabbed me hard around the waist, burying his face in my chest.

"I missed you, Dad," I said.

TWENTY-THREE

EVEN THOUGH I WAS TIRED from chopping and stacking firewood I couldn't sleep for the longest time. My mind was going full tilt, like those big computer banks in the old sci-fi movies, different-coloured lights flashing without a rest.

I couldn't get up and watch the tube the way I'd do at home because the TV was too close to the bedroom—everything in Sharon's house was close to everything else—and I'd wake Dad and Sharon up. I figured they both deserved some rest. Dad was pretty wrung-out and Sharon must have been, too.

So I lay there and thrashed around, bashing my pillow a thousand times, twisting the bedding into a tangle, getting more and more frustrated trying to fall asleep. Finally I gave up and let the thoughts run.

For the first time in my life I thought about how hard it must have been for my father when he left home. He had wandered all over North America, it seemed like. I wondered about the places he had been to, how he had supported himself—any kind of job he could pick up, I guessed. There were lots of things I didn't know about him. Ten years' worth of things. Like, how do you fake not being able to read or write? How do you fake it so well that even your wife and kid don't know?

I'm not saying my mind was full of warm happy thoughts about him. Like I told him, I didn't know if I'd ever be able to forgive him for leaving. I knew the reasons now, but that didn't make the hurt go away. Explaining stuff doesn't always make it better.

Now there was someone else to be mad at. My mother. It was pretty cruel, what she did to him and to me. Because there was no doubt that, if a divorce judge had asked me when I was seven who I wanted to live with, I know who I'd have picked. Maybe she knew that, knew she might lose her little boy, and that's why she threatened him.

I remember one time in English when Ms. Cake told us—I forget why—the Bible story of the two women who were fighting over a baby. Each woman claimed the kid was hers, and they went to court to get a decision. Solomon, the crafty king-judge, said the only thing to do was cut the baby in two and give each woman half a kid. Then they'd both be satisfied.

One woman said, great idea. But, the other one was horrified. She said no, she changed her mind, it wasn't her baby after all. Solomon knew then that she was the real mother, and he awarded the kid to her.

Well, nice story, but that's all it was—a story. Real life didn't work that way. In real life people would say yeah, cut him up. Then they'd argue about who got the biggest piece.

Parents. They teach you not to be selfish, but when it comes to losing something they can be worse than kids. Except we have to admit it and they don't.

I rolled over for the thousandth time and punched my pillow again, wishing I could punch both my parents that easily.

Oh, hell, I thought, what makes you so perfect, Wick? It was just a big tragedy for everybody. There was nobody to blame. It was funny in a way. It was nobody's fault, but everybody got hurt anyway, everybody got cut in half. And everybody was alone—a seven-year-old who didn't know what was going on; his mother, working like a mad-woman to be a big success, living up to her parents' standards, with no husband or social life; his father, wandering around by himself, sending postcards he couldn't write on to a son he couldn't visit.

Loneliness, I realized, is the worst feeling in the world, worse than pain, worse than anything. Especially when no one else understands, when no one else seems to care.

And then, as if someone had slammed me in the back of the head with one of the slabs of firewood I had cut that afternoon, it hit me—the terrible isolation and loneliness that Hawk must have felt that day in the shower room when he told me his secret. There I was, rambling on inside my head about how my father had left me rather than face up to his illiteracy, feeling mad at him, saying I wasn't sure I could forgive him. And what had I done to Hawk?

"The same damn thing," I said aloud. "Worse. A lot worse." My voice bounced off the walls in the dark room, accusing me. I was his best friend, and when he told me his deepest secret, when he needed me most, I had run off and left him blubbering in the corner of the shower room.

I got out of bed and went to the phone. I punched in the Toronto area code, then Hawk's number.

It rang about eight times and I was about to hang up when someone answered.

"Hello?" It was Hawk's voice, and yet it wasn't. It was weak and timid, the voice of a grade one kid talking to the principal.

I stood paralyzed, wondering what to say. Think of something! I told myself. I took a deep breath.

"Stop doing this!" Hawk screamed before I could talk. "Leave me alone! I've had enough, you bastards!" He slammed down the phone.

I stood there staring at the receiver until it sank in that he hadn't known it was me. Who did he think it was? Then I knew. All the guys on the wrestling team had seen the pictures. It would have been all over the school the next day. Hawk Richardson is gay. The Athlete of the Year is a fag.

And Wick Chandler is his best friend.

TWENTY-FOUR

I SPENT THE NEXT FEW DAYS moping around, not doing much. My father went into town to his show twice a day—he came back to Sharon's for lunch—and sometimes I went with him and hung around the mall. That got boring after a while, though. Sometimes I cut firewood for Sharon. I mowed the lawn for her, which would have made my mother die of shock if she ever found out. Sharon's smile was hard to resist, though.

I had a couple of good talks with Sharon. Once, as we sat in lawn chairs in the shade of the oak tree in her yard, she told me about how she met my father. It had happened a little over five years before, in Sault Ste. Marie. She had been working in an arts and crafts store just north of the city and he had come in, peddling his sculptures. They talked a bit, she said, and he came back the next day. And the day after that.

"What attracted me to your dad was his gentleness," she said. "You know, this town is full of macho types, full of swagger and loud talk. Your dad isn't like that."

I asked her why they didn't live together permanently.

"He hasn't been able to settle down, Wick, and I'm not going to force him. Used to be, he just wanted to be on the move. But now he's an established artist. Not famous, but he's becoming known in certain places. So now he has to do a certain amount of travelling. But he isn't gone for very long, and he always comes back here. Besides, I have an idea that he'll find it easier to settle down now."

"I hope so," I said.

"I do too. Because when—or if—he does, I'm going to take another whack at getting him to go back to school."

I pictured my father in a classroom slouching in his chair with his moccasined feet stuck out in the aisle, puffing on his pipe and mumbling comments to himself while the teacher rambled on about verbs and nouns.

"That would be great," I said, "but do you think he'd go?"

"I don't know. I've tried to get him to sign up with one of those literacy programs you see advertised in the paper every now and then. But so far he's resisted. Says he's too busy, but that's only part of it. He still has a lot of anger inside about his experiences in school. And before he goes back to school he has to admit to other people that he has a problem. Your dad's an awfully proud man, Wick."

"Sharon, do you mind if I ask you something else?"

"Go ahead."

"How did you find out?"

She shrugged. "Well, after we discovered we loved each other, he told me there was something I should know before we got real serious. Said he'd made a big mistake once and he wasn't going to make it again. I was expecting him to say he had a drug problem or that he'd been in jail, anything but the fact that he couldn't read or write. I was the first person he'd ever admitted it to." She smiled. "You're the second, Wick."

"But ... don't take this wrong, but didn't it change the way you thought of him?"

"I was shocked, naturally—I mean, he hid it so well. But, no, it didn't change anything between us. He's the same man I fell in love with."

To keep in shape I did my exercises and went for a run every morning. I was getting nervous again about the meet and didn't want to lose my training edge. The problem was, the exercises made me think of Hawk, since we almost always did them together at school, and the runs gave me too much time to think. Running is great if you want to get away from everyone and think about something, maybe thrash out a problem, but when you don't want to think, running is a drag.

A dozen times I picked up the phone to call Hawk, and a dozen times I put it down again.

TWENTY-FIVE

EARLY MONDAY MORNING we said goodbye to Sharon and left for Thunder Bay. Dad had got the van tuned up—he sold a lot of sculptures over the weekend and had a few bucks to spend—and replaced the muffler himself. I told him if he was going to play opera on the stereo it might be better to have the muffler the way it was.

The Trans–Canada Highway took us up the east shore of Lake Superior. The mountains and the lake combined to produce some terrific scenery, with sweeping deep blue bays and mountainous peninsulas. My father seemed to know where he was going. I asked him if he had been this way before and he said yes.

"But what about the first time?" I asked. "I mean, how do you find your way around?" Another thought struck me. "And how did you find your way around in all the travelling you did?"

He didn't say anything at first and I began to wonder if I had embarrassed him. "Do you mind me asking you?"

"I guess if you'd asked me a couple weeks ago I'd've said yes, but now it's kind of a relief, bein' able to talk about it. Hidin' stuff is high pressure, you know?

"If you can't read, you've gotta get by with word of mouth, you've gotta ask directions all the time. People naturally tell me street names, thinkin' I'll find the signs, so I ask them about landmarks—you know, a gas station or a big grey building, whatever. I can read numbers, as long as they're not too long, so I can follow a map because all the highways are numbered. If I'm goin' somewhere, I count the towns I'll pass through on the way. Then when I think I'm where I want to be, I stop at a gas station or a restaurant and shoot the breeze for a few minutes and then say, 'What town is this, anyway? I missed the sign.'" He smiled around the stem of his pipe. "You get to meet a lot of people that way.

"If somebody gives me somethin' to read," he went on, "I tell them I forgot my glasses. I usually carry an empty glasses case in my pocket. That works most of the time. At the show, there, back in the Soo, I did the glasses routine quite a bit, told the gallery people Sharon was my business manager and acted the part of the hare-brained artist who doesn't understand worldly things like bills or money or commissions."

He chuckled, and held the steering wheel tightly while a huge transport truck loaded with logs roared past, shaking the van like a paper box, but his laugh had a bitter edge to it.

"In school I failed grade one and two. 'Course, they didn't hold me back. I went on to the next grade. I knew I'd failed, and all the other kids knew, and the teacher pretended I hadn't, but I had.

"So, you know, I felt kind of bad about myself. I didn't have no confidence. No matter how hard I tried, nothin' seemed to work. One of my teachers used to get on my case, tellin' me I had a lazy mind. I guess I don't blame her now. It must've been awful frustratin', tryin' to get me to read and write.

"Anyway, feelin' bad about myself like that, I got into a lot of trouble. Fights, talkin' back to the teachers, not doin' any work because I couldn't write. The usual. Things didn't change too much when they finally pushed me into high school. I earned some credits in the couple of years I was there—arts, phys ed, a few shops. But I spent most of my time skippin' classes, and when I turned sixteen I was gone.

"See, even though school was failure after failure, inside I knew I was better than that. I knew I could draw—it was the only time I ever got good marks in elementary school—and I knew I wasn't stupid. But most of the time I felt lonely. I felt like I was standin' on the outside of a high chain-link fence, and I could see all the other kids, all the other adults, playin', workin', gettin' along with a normal life, but I couldn't get in. I still can't. It isn't like the gate's locked. It's like there isn't a gate at all."

He struck a match on the underside of the steering column and lit his pipe, then stuffed the match into the pile of other matches in the ashtray.

"So anyways," he said through a cloud of smoke, "what the hell. After I quit school I got along. I found jobs. If I had to fill out an application I'd take it home and get my mom to help me with it. Or I'd go after jobs where they'd just as soon pay you under the table, so there was no application. Thing is, though, all those jobs were the same—lousy pay and no benefits. And every day you're thinkin', is this the day they're goin' to find out about me and fire me?

"After I left you and your mother and I was on the road, I picked up enough work to pay for food and gas and I kept on the move. Did a little stealin', too, when I had to. I knew by then that I wanted to really work on my carvin' and I started to offer some pieces for sale at tourist shops and places like that. They'd buy them from me and mark up the price. I never stayed around long enough to know what happened to them, but I made sure my mark was carved onto the base of every damn one of them."

We drove along for a while. My mind was going a million miles a minute, swirling with questions, but I didn't want to fire a barrage of How-did-you-do-thats at him. Instead I watched the scenery crawl past and let my mind run.

It amazed me that my mother never found out until that night at her office party. I guessed she would have handled all their money—writing the cheques, going to the bank, all that stuff—because, knowing her, she would have wanted to anyway. And when you think of it, how often do parents write each other notes?

But what about the million other things in life that required the ability to read and write? I had never thought about it—who does?—but everything in my life assumed reading and writing. How do you look up the baseball and hockey scores in the newspaper? How do you check out the TV guide to see what's on when you feel like crashing in front of the tube at night? How do you find your favourite group in the record store, and make sure you don't buy the same CD you bought last time? For that matter, how do you find the record store? Suppose you meet a great-looking girl and you want to look up her number in the phone book. You'd be out of luck.

I remembered one day in English when Ms. Cake gave us a journal topic, something like "How would your life be different if you were illiterate?" We sat there looking mystified and most of us wrote dumb stuff like "I wouldn't be able to read Stephen King novels" or smart-ass things like "I wouldn't be able to do my English homework." In the discussion that followed, Cake was very earnest, but we just joked around. Now it didn't seem so funny. And now the word *illiterate*, which I always thought meant you were stupid, didn't sound so scientific.

"Hey, Dad," I burst out, "how did you ever get a driver's licence?"

"What makes you think I've got one? No, relax," he added, laughing, "I'm legal. A long time ago I found a nice lady—after I tried this trick at a half dozen Ministry of Transport offices—who believed me when I told her I lost my glasses. I convinced her to read the questions for me and I answered orally. Got all the answers right, too. The road test was easy. See, I can tell what all the signs say by the colour and shape and where they are. You know, a sign with kids on it holding books, something like that. It isn't hard. And I can write my name and all. I draw it. But it looks like a five-year-old wrote it, so most of the time I try to get away without signin' things."

Yeah, like postcards, I thought. No signature.

"Sharon's been after me to take a shot at one of them literacy classes. But, I don't know." He geared down as the van struggled up a long hill. "Don't forget, Steve, humans got along great for thousands of years without bein' able to read and write. People like me are like them. We learn to use our ears, and we gotta have a good memory." He tapped his temple with the stem of his pipe. "We gotta store a lot of information up here." He paused. "Sure is a pain in the butt sometimes, though."

I remembered what he had said about being on the wrong side of the fence with no gate. He must have suffered a thousand defeats when he was a kid at school, a million humiliations. He must have lost out on a lot. Including his family.

"She shouldn't have done it," I thought, pounding my fist on my thigh.

"What's that, Steve?"

"Nothing," I said. "I was just thinking out loud."

TWENTY-SIX

LONG BEFORE WE SAW ANY BUILDINGS the stink from the pulp mills told us we were getting close to Thunder Bay. I had a map on my lap and squinted into the late-afternoon sun that slanted crossways into the van, looking for road signs.

The university wasn't very big but it was modern, with attractive buildings done in a sand-coloured brick. The campus was mostly open land with wide lawns, carefully tended shrubs and lots of parking. When we got out of the van and looked behind us we could see the Sleeping Giant across the harbour.

My father and I went into the main building, the University Centre, and found the registration desk in a large foyer. There were lots of athletes there already, strutting around in track suits with logos of their schools or clubs on them. I didn't see anyone I knew. I hadn't been too nervous up to now—so much had gone in the last nine days—but the sight of the other wrestlers, the sound of their banter, and the serious looks behind the jokes really wound me up. I registered, was handed a thick folder full of information and a map of the university, and was pointed toward the residence where my room was.

We skirted Tamblyn Lake, a small pond that the buildings were grouped around, and followed a stone

137

path to the Prettie Residence. After a few minutes walking up and down the halls we found the room.

It was small, on the second floor, looking over the so-called lake. There were two single beds.

"Well," I said to my father, "looks like there's room for both of us."

He was looking around as if he had landed on Mars. "Finally," he said with a laugh, "I made it to university! Now I can tell people, 'Yep, I went to Lakehead U.' I don't have to tell them it was only for two days."

TWENTY-SEVEN

I GOT UP EARLY TUESDAY and went for an easy run while my father went out for doughnuts and coffee. I came back to the main facility just before eight o'clock for the weigh-in. The place was thronged with wrestlers, some outfitted in the latest threads, some going the other way, wearing worn grey track suits with holes in the knees and cut-off arms. I was hoping they paid less attention to training than their looks.

After the weigh-in I went into the third double gym to stretch and warm up. It was packed with wrestlers of all sizes, and the racket from their talk and laughter bounced off the walls.

Keeping to myself, I got to work stretching on the mat, then went to the wall for back-arches, starting easy and building to full arches, then a crab walk. Usually while I'm warming up I also psych up—get my mind in gear, get aggressive. You have to believe you can win, that you can make your opponent pay every time he pulls a move on you. And you've got to go to the mat ready to rock 'n' roll. You can't wander into the gym and shake hands with your opponent thinking, Gee, I sure hope I'll do okay. The guy'll kill you.

But I kept thinking about Hawk, and I couldn't get psyched. I should have called him back, I knew. I had chickened out. I had been afraid, not knowing what to say to the new Hawk, the one I now knew was gay. Try psyching yourself up, telling yourself you're a mean strong machine on the mat, powerful, crafty and fast—try it when you really know you're a coward.

I went to the foyer to check my match time and pool, feeling more like a limp piece of string than a powerhouse. I was on at nine o'clock. Good, I thought, get started early so there's no time to stand around letting the jitters sap your energy. I went to the change room and put on my red singlet and the new Nikes my mother had bought me to bring good luck. As I double-knotted the stiff white laces I promised myself I'd call Hawk that night and tell him how I did, who I'd face the next day in the medal rounds. If I made it to the second day.

The first match went okay. My opponent wasn't in as good shape as he should have been, and when he realized I was a lot stronger than him he got dirty. He cross-faced me a couple of times in the second round, and that got me mad. I paid him back with a painful gut-wrench, then, after we tied up again, I threw him. He landed like a bag of wet sand and I pinned him.

The ref took us to centre and held my hand in the air. Someone in the stands was stomping his feet and cheering like a retard.

I'll bet he never hollered like that at the opera.

TWENTY-EIGHT

MY OPPONENT FOR THE SECOND match was a black kid, strong and fit, and a lot tougher than the first guy. But my concentration began to return and I was able to rack up points using gut-wrenches and ankle locks on him. By the end of the round the score was 8–2. In the middle of the second round the match was stopped because I beat him on technical superiority.

The third match, after lunch, just about killed me. The opponent was a kid I had fought before in Toronto. He was as strong as Hercules—at least it seemed that way on the mat—but, lucky for me, he wasn't very fast. That's where I got it over him. But he made me pay. I beat him by one point and by the time I was finished I was exhausted.

The last match of the day found me still tired. I hoped my opponent was more tired than me. He was shorter than me, a white guy, very hairy.

He caught me asleep early on and I was almost pinned. From then on I fought defensively, using the zone a lot, waiting until he moved on me and then trying to score on counter-moves. The score was even when the final round was almost over.

Then I tried something I do once in a while. I had been wrestling pretty defensively, like I said, and the guy got too used to it. When we had tied up and worked our way near the zone, pushing and shoving, I wound up all the strength I had left and exploded. I locked my hands behind his head, stepped in deep, pivoted and threw him. Talk about airborne. As he smashed to the mat in the out-of-bounds area I caught a glimpse of the ref holding up three fingers.

When we tied up again at centre I just kept away for the remaining seconds. I picked up a caution for passivity, but it didn't matter by then. I was glad to hear the buzzer and see the big yellow sponge sail into the ring to mark the end of the match.

Four wins! Suddenly I didn't feel tired any more.

Back in our room, I came out of the shower to hear my father on the phone. He was just saying goodbye.

"Love you too," he said in a low voice, his back to me.

He cracked open a beer and threw himself into a chair, looking real happy about something. "Man, what a day for the Chandlers! First you win four in a row—that means you're in the medal rounds tomorrow, right?—and I get an offer on a sculpture that would knock your socks off!"

"Which one?" I asked, towelling my hair.

"The one I did for you, the wrestlers."

My exhilaration drained away. "Oh, yeah?" I said, trying to hide my disappointment. "A good offer?"

"How's ten thousand bucks sound? That's the best offer by far I've ever had. Some character who runs a sports equipment outfit in the States wants to buy it. He wants to put it in a case in the lobby of their buildin'."

"So it's gone?" I said.

"Are you kiddin'? No way I sell that one. That one's not for sale."

Well, I felt pretty good that night. We went out to an Italian restaurant and oinked out on pasta, then caught an early movie, a real dog about some macho types rescuing a beautiful but dumb woman captured by terrorists. I fidgeted all through the flick, knowing what I had to do when we returned to our room.

As soon as we were back in the dorm I forced myself to pick up the phone. Taking a deep breath I punched in Hawk's number. I figured I'd just play it cool, tell him about the matches, act as if everything was normal.

"Hello?" It was Hawk's mother.

"Hi, Mrs. Richardson, it's Wick."

"Oh, hello, Wick. How are you?" Her voice was lifeless and sad.

"Um, fine. I'm in Thunder Bay at the meet. Is Hawk there?"

"He . . . isn't here now, Wick."

"Oh. When will he be back?"

There was a long pause. "Malcolm is . . . Malcolm is in the hospital, Wick."

"Why?" I asked, suddenly afraid, "What's the matter?"

"He was almost killed last night. He crashed the car."

Through the telephone line the crying started.

TWENTY-NINE

"YOU LOOK LIKE YOU'VE SEEN A GHOST." My father stood in the middle of the room, his beer in his hand, an anxious look on his face.

"It's Hawk," I said, putting the phone down and lowering myself slowly into a chair. My hands shook and my throat had suddenly gone dry.

"It's what? I don't get you."

I tried to assemble the bits of information that Hawk's mother had given me, bits that ricocheted around inside my skull, resisting any sort of order. "My friend Hawk smashed up the car. He's in the hospital. She said he almost died, that he's on the critical list."

My father sat in the chair opposite me. "What happened?"

"She . . . she said he hit a bridge on the Gardiner Expressway. She said he was drunk."

I knew the exact place. Hawk had been going west on the Gardiner and had taken the exit ramp to the Lakeshore. That ramp goes off to the right, then curves in a giant S under the bridge before it joins the Lakeshore. Hawk had missed the first curve of the S and slammed into the massive concrete bridge abutment, head-on, with enough speed to demolish the Richardsons' little Toyota.

"He did it on purpose," I said.

144

"She said that?"

"No, she probably didn't realize. But I know it. He tried to kill himself."

My father took a pull on his beer, hesitated, then passed it to me. "Take a drink, Steve, it'll help to calm you down."

I did as he said, forcing the cool suds down my throat. The drink seemed to help me get my breath. I handed it back to him.

"Keep it," he said. "I'll get another one." He went to the little fridge. As he popped the new can open he asked, "What . . . how do you know he did it on purpose?"

"Because Hawk never drinks. One summer after we finished grade nine he and I got drunk. We just wanted to try the stuff. The next day he was so sick he vowed he'd never drink again. And he never did."

"Maybe he fell off the wagon, like they say."

"No, not him. Besides, he's an absolute fanatic about seatbelts. He never drives without it on, never rides in someone else's car without his seatbelt on. He won't let you drive with him unless you wear yours."

My father was silent awhile. Then he said, "Why would he try to kill himself?"

I told my father about what I had discovered in the locker room. How I had abandoned Hawk when he needed me. How I should have known from the phone call I had made from Sharon's house that he was being harassed by other kids. How I should have done something then.

"I was only worried about myself," I said bitterly, "and what people would think about *me*. I never considered him."

145

"Steve," my father said gently, "it's not your fault."

"I let him down, Dad. I should have been there for him."

"Yeah, you did let him down. But you didn't pour the liquor down his throat. You didn't put him in the car."

I shook my head.

"Look, Steve, I know what I'm talkin' about. It's like me and the booze. Quite a few years ago, I had it real bad. I seemed to be drunk all the time. I had all the excuses in the world to drink. It was always somebody else's fault. Then after I met Sharon she helped me see that no matter how hurt I was, it was me makin' the decision to try to run away into a bottle. It was me, no one else. This friend of yours, he's suffered a helluva lot. We'll never know, probably, how much pain he's been through. But he's the one who chose how to handle the pain."

"Dad, I let him down," I said again.

"Okay, fine. You did. But most people in your situation would have acted the same way. Don't you think so?"

I thought about the other guys I know. How we had all grown up the same way, killing off parts of ourselves so we'd be hard and tough, so nobody could ever accuse us of the ultimate sin.

"Maybe," I said.

"So don't think about what you didn't do then. Think about how you can help him now."

"Dad, I want to go back to Toronto to see him. Will you take me?"

"What about the tournament? You could win the gold."

"I don't care about that now."

My father smiled. He came over to me and put his hand on my shoulder. "I figured you'd say that."

THIRTY

WE PULLED INTO SAULT STE. MARIE at about 3:00 a.m., picked up Sharon, and hit the road again. Exhausted by the tournament and the long drive from Thunder Bay, I sacked out in the back seat.

I woke up to the sounds of traffic on the highway. It was boiling hot inside the van and my mouth felt thick and sticky. The sun was high in the sky.

Sharon swung west onto the 401, changing lanes jerkily as we merged with the traffic. We took the 427 south and then, a few miles farther on, the exit ramp to the Queensway. I soon saw the blue signs with the white H on them that indicated a hospital ahead. We stopped at a light and I could see the Queensway General, across the road from Sherway Shopping Centre. Sharon turned into the parking lot and took a ticket from the machine.

"Want me to come in with you?" my father said.

I felt a pain in the pit of my stomach. Now that we were there, I didn't want to go in.

"No thanks," I said.

"Why don't we go across to the mall there and get a bite to eat?" Sharon suggested to my father.

"Uh, yeah, good idea. I'm starved."

We got out of the van. "We'll meet you here later, Steve," my father said, squinting against the bright sun.

"Okay."

Before they left, Sharon put her arms around me and squeezed hard. "Everything will be okay, Wick," she said.

"Yeah," I said, certain she was wrong.

Inside, the hospital was cool and dark. At the information counter I asked the woman where Hawk's room was, then followed her directions along gloomy corridors that smelled of unnamed chemicals. An old man dressed in a ratty brown bathrobe shuffled by me in slippered feet, pushing a wheeled IV stand along in front of him. I passed a nursing station. One nurse was on the phone, another was writing on a clip-board, while a candy-striper poured orange juice into paper cups lined up on a tray. I turned another corner, passed a room in which someone was yelling "Ah! Ah!" in a long painful wail that set my nerves further on edge.

At the end of the corridor, just past another nursing station, I saw a closed door. It was Hawk's room. I took a deep breath and put my hand on the door to push it open.

"Can I help you?" came a voice behind me.

The nurse was tall, her coal-black skin contrasting with the crisp white of her uniform. She held a chrome tray in one hand. On it, a hypodermic needle lay on a small towel beside a tiny bottle.

"I'm here to see Hawk."

"Who?"

"Uh, Malcolm Richardson."

"Are you a relative?"

"I'm . . . " I'm his best friend, I was going to say, but the words stuck in my throat. "Yeah, a cousin."

"Well you can't go in now. I'm just about to give him a shot. You can wait over there."

149

She pointed to a couple of chairs set before a window. I went over and looked out onto the lawns and garden at the back of the hospital.

The door opened a moment later and Hawk's mother came out. She paused as the door hissed shut behind her. She took a tissue from her purse and dabbed her eyes, then put the tissue back into the purse and snapped it shut. Her face was drawn and tight.

She hadn't seen me. I wanted to greet her, but I was afraid I'd blurt out that it was my fault her son tried to kill himself.

She walked down the hall away from me. I let her go.

THIRTY-ONE

THE NURSE CAME OUT of Hawk's room about five minutes later and told me I could go in, but I couldn't stay long.

The semi-private room was warm and dark and silent. A floor-length curtain was drawn around the first bed and something inside hissed and gurgled. The figure in the second bed could have been anybody.

Hawk's right leg was encased in a heavy plaster cast and hung suspended from a rack attached to the side of the bed frame. His left arm, also in a cast from shoulder to fingers, rested across his chest. The inside of his right forearm was bruised and yellowed where an IV needle was taped to his skin. Hawk's head was wrapped in bandages down to his eyebrows, and a few stitches puckered the scraped skin between his eyes and on the bridge of his nose. His eyes were closed and his chest rose and fell.

I stood there, looking at him, wondering if he was asleep. "Hawk, it's me," I finally whispered, reluctant to break the stillness of the room. I cleared my throat and said, louder this time, "It's Wick."

I thought I saw his eyelids twitch just a little, but I couldn't be sure. I moved to his side. "Hey, Hawk, are you awake?" I whispered.

His eyes remained closed. His chest rose and fell with the same peaceful rhythm. Maybe the dope the nurse gave him put him out, I thought, and some of the tension eased from my limbs.

The silence was broken only by the gurgles and hisses from behind the curtain. I looked Hawk over. He sure had done it to himself. In spite of what my father had said to me, I still felt guilty, still felt responsible for the cuts and bruises and cracked bones. And yet his body, the body that wanted to do things with other men, repelled me. I couldn't get my mind around that cold hard fact, and I knew I probably never would. There was no use trying to run away from that. But he was still my friend and I knew that the agony he felt inside was worse than the pain of his wounds.

I forced myself to touch him. I knew I had to, or I would never touch him again. Carefully, so as not to hurt—or waken—him, I laid my hand on his shoulder, moved it slowly across the rough cloth of his hospital gown until one of my fingers touched his neck. His skin was warm, and his pulse beat against my fingertip. "I'm sorry, Hawk," I whispered.

Then I left the room. In the hall I asked the nurse how he was. She told me he was no longer critical, that eventually he would mend. Beyond that she couldn't say.

"He's in a deep sleep," I told her.

"That's funny," she said. "He was awake when I left him."

THIRTY-TWO

I MADE MY WAY THROUGH the hospital corridors. As I passed through the lobby the elevator doors opened and two men stepped out. One was grey-haired and he was crying. The other was younger, his son maybe, and he had his arm around the old man's shoulder, comforting him.

I was glad to get out into the sunlight again, even though it was hot. Sharon and my father weren't back from lunch yet. The van sat baking in the heat. The red patches where my father had repaired the body work looked like wounds against the faded white paint.

Out on the lawn there were three benches arranged in the shade of a big maple. I sat down at the one that faced away from the hospital and watched the traffic. Buses snorted along, belching diesel smoke. The passengers sat in the heat ignoring each other, staring into nowhere. Cars hurried along, the sun reflecting off tinted windows.

I didn't blame Hawk for pretending to be asleep. It had made it easier for both of us. If he hadn't pretended, I wouldn't have touched him.

I wished I was five years old again so I could cry all the confusing emotions out of me. Instead, I sat there under the maple, wrestling with my feelings and losing on points. Girls were allowed to cry in front of people, I thought, but we weren't. Girls were allowed to go *Oooooh* and *Ahhhh* when they saw something cute or sweet, or touch each other, hug each other, but we weren't. We all did what Hawk had done. We pretended that a big part of us wasn't there.

I realized now—Hawk had known it all along—that the way a lot of guys talked about girls, as if they were meat, as if they were toys you used when you wanted to, was all a cover. They were afraid to treat girls like people because in girls they saw the part of themselves that they had been taught to kill.

I had been no different. I remembered how embarrassed I had been at the opera when my father had cried. And I had pretended not to know him because he was a man and he had broken one of the big rules.

Thinking of my father and Hawk like that, watching the cars carry their solitary occupants along the road, I wondered how many of those strangers out on the street held secrets inside them, and if any held secrets as terrible as Hawk's and my father's. Terrible because, if they came out into the sunlight, people would use them to tear you down. Illiterate, gay—both meant, people thought, that something was wrong with you.

I used to think so, too.

I got up off the bench and went back into the hospital.

THIRTY-THREE

HAWK'S NURSE WAS BUSY in the nursing station, with her back to the corridor, so I slipped into his room. The first bed was still curtained off, but the window drapes had been pulled aside, allowing the afternoon light to flood the room.

Hawk's head was propped up by three or four pillows. He was watching a little TV that swung out over the bed on a bracket. He had earphones plugged into his ears.

His eyes widened in surprise when he saw me at the foot of the bed. With his good hand he slowly removed the earphones and pushed the TV aside. A ball game was on. Tiny players flickered across the screen, attempting a double-play.

"Jays are losing again," Hawk said in a voice that seemed slow and heavy. Probably the dope, I thought.

"Oh," I said. Then, "How's the food?"

"Don't know. Can't eat yet."

"Oh. Yeah. Right."

There was a long pause. Both of us watched the commercial on the screen. A bunch of athletic-looking guys wearing tight jeans and checked shirts were standing on a dock trying to decide whether to go fishing or drink some more beer first.

"Well, this conversation's going real good, isn't it?"

I smiled. "Yeah."

Another long pause.

"I'm glad you know, Wick."

"Yeah."

"I hope it doesn't make too much difference."

I couldn't lie to him. I wasn't exactly looking forward to being known as a gay's best friend. So I settled for, "I'm here, Hawk. I'm not leaving again. Not unless you want me to."

Silence.

"It's gonna be hard, though," he said. "Everybody knows now."

"How did you parents take it?"

"They've known for a long time."

Hawk's eyes switched to the TV again, so I looked too. Another ad. A well-dressed guy with thick hands and a firm jaw drove a sleek-looking red sports car up to a stoplight. Three women in tight dresses admired the car, then smiled seductively at the guy. The car was called Intimidator.

Hawk spoke again, his voice thick with bitterness. "I should change my name from Hawk to Half-man."

"Hawk, listen—"

"No, I'm serious. I'm so short I'm half a man. I'm gay, so I'm half woman."

"You never took any shit from anyone about your size, Hawk."

"Damn right."

"So . . . "

"Yeah. This will be harder, though."

"Your parents are with you. So am I."

"It's gonna be hard for you, too, Wick." Hawk

may not have been a scholar, but he wasn't stupid either.

"I know it is."

"I'll understand if . . . "

"Forget it, Hawk."

There was another long pause.

"Want to watch the game for a while?"

"Sure," I said.

I pulled a chair up to the bed and leaned over, my arm resting on the bed beside Hawk. He took one earphone and I took the other. At the eighth inning the nurse came in with her trusty tray. She asked what I was doing there. Hawk wasn't supposed to have any visitors.

"Your cousin will have to leave," she said to Hawk.

Hawk looked at me and smirked. "See you later, Cuz," he said.

THIRTY-FOUR

MY FATHER AND SHARON dropped me off at home that afternoon, then went to find a motel. They had decided to stay in Toronto for a few days, to spend some of his earnings from his show in the Soo, they said, visit the art galleries, go to the symphony, see some new movies. But I knew he wanted to stick around because of me.

Just as he turned down our street Sharon said, "Wick, your dad and I would like to invite you to spend the rest of the summer with us in the Soo. What do you think?"

"I don't know, Sharon, all that opera and cowboy music?" I joked.

My father laughed and said around the stem of his pipe, "It'll take at least the summer to get some musical taste banged into that shaved head of yours. Anyway, Steve, we'd really like to have you with us."

"Thanks, Dad, I'd like to, but I want to stick around with Hawk. For a few weeks, anyway."

I hoped he wouldn't be disappointed. Instead, he smiled. "I figured you'd say that. Here is where you probably should be. How about we agree that you'll come up for at least two weeks toward the end of the summer."

"Great," I said.

Before my mother came home—I had called her at the office from the hospital to tell her I was back—I mowed the lawn, vacuumed the pool and even cleaned up my room. Strange behaviour for me but, to tell the truth, I did the work to keep from thinking about my mother. I failed, naturally. You can't ask yourself not to think about something.

While I worked I kept trying to convince myself that my mother had only done what she thought was best. That laying blame wasn't going to change anything. That she had been lonely, too. That all three of us had suffered in one way or another.

But believing something in your head isn't the same as believing it in your heart. Telling myself all those things didn't dull the anger. While I was putting away the lawn mower I laughed bitterly because I realized that the deep rage I had felt toward my father for all those years wasn't gone at all. It was still there, like a constant, painful pressure behind my eyeballs, only now it was directed at my mother.

Later on, around seven, I was standing at the window of my room when I saw her walking slowly down the street, bent a little sideways with the weight of her briefcase.

When I came into the kitchen she was sitting at the table groping around in her purse. She was wearing a pink dress with a broad white belt and a pearl necklace. Against the bright material of the dress her skin was pale. She looked up at me, shaking a cigarette from the pack. As she lit it her hands trembled.

We both waited for the other to break the tension that stretched between us like a steel band. She took a long drag, letting the smoke out slowly.

"Have a nice trip?"

Seeing her there, her shoulders slumped with fatigue, her face fearful, her hand shaking as she brought the cigarette to her pale lips, I held back my anger.

"It was okay."

She offered a thin smile. "That's nice."

"Mom, he told me everything," I said evenly.

"You mean—"

"Everything."

She started to cry silently. She stubbed out her half-finished cigarette, rose, and took a tissue from a box on the counter. Leaning on the counter, she wiped her eyes.

"I'm sorry," she said.

So there it was. Half of me wanted to hug her, tell her it was okay. The other half wanted to shout, to pound the words out. Being sorry is meaningless. It doesn't change anything.

"You ought to be," I said. "He didn't deserve what you did to him. Neither did I."

"I'm so sorry," she whispered.

"Yeah, well, I guess there's nothing anybody can do about it now."

Later, after my mother had showered and changed, we zapped a couple of TV dinners in the micro and ate out on the patio. There was a cool breeze off the lake, and we could see what seemed like thousands of boats in the distance, their sails illuminated by the setting sun.

Over dinner I told her about the wrestling meet and about Hawk's accident. That's how I described it— an accident.

"Steve, before you went up north, remember Hawk called and you refused to talk to him? What was all that about? It wasn't like you to treat him like that."

So I laid it all out for her. Her face went white.

"My god," she said, putting down her cup. "His parents must be devastated."

"They've known for a long time, Mom. They'll handle it okay."

"My god," she said again. "I don't know if *I* can. What will I say to him when he comes over?"

"Try 'Hi, Hawk.'"

"That's not amusing, Steve."

"Well, he's the same guy, Mom."

She didn't ask about my father, but I told her about him anyway—his show, the sculpture of me wrestling. I wasn't sure how she'd like the idea of him and me getting along. When I said I wanted to go up to the Soo for a couple of weeks before school started up again she didn't look too pleased.

"Well, I guess it's your decision, Stevie."

"That's right, Mom, it is. I have two parents, now."

She flushed a little, as if she'd been caught without her make-up on. She looked like she was about to say something. Instead, she took a sip of coffee and looked out over the lake.

Pretty soon she grew restless and went inside to her study to do some work. I cleared the table and loaded the dishwasher.

THIRTY-FIVE

OVER THE NEXT WEEK OR SO I went to see Hawk every day. My father and Sharon picked me up each afternoon and dropped me off at the hospital. Hawk and I would watch a ball game on the little TV, or I'd read while he slept. He slept a lot. It was pretty boring in that hospital.

According to his doctor, Hawk was healing well. He had a bunch of months to go before he was anywhere near normal but it looked good. One thing still bothered me, though. How was Hawk doing *inside?* He seemed to be coping okay, but I wondered if, when he got out of the hospital, he'd fall into a deep depression again and try to hurt himself.

One day I wound up my courage and said, "Hawk, do you . . . do you ever feel like trying it again?"

He seemed to know what I meant. "You don't need to worry about that, Wick."

"Promise?"

"I was just trying to get revenge."

"On who?" I gulped. "Me?"

"No, no. Not you. On life, I guess."

"I read somewhere that suicide is the ultimate temper tantrum," I said.

He laughed. "Yeah, that's about it."

He was worried that he'd never be able to do sports again, but his doctor seemed optimistic about his chances. Although he'd be out of commission for at least a year, Hawk would probably be able to wrestle again. That perked him up a lot. He and I figured he could help the Fanatic with the coaching next year.

"I can teach the new cadets how to Go Animal," Hawk said.

THIRTY-SIX

MY FATHER CALLED ME A FEW DAYS later and told me he and Sharon were heading back north the next day. "I'm getting itchy feet," he said. "Too long in one place. Especially the city. The noise and pollution are startin' to get to me."

Before they left, they wanted me to go out for dinner with them. "And I've got a surprise," he added. "Dress up."

"Like you?" I joked.

He laughed and hung up.

When they picked me up my father was wearing a sports coat and pants that didn't say Levi's on them. Sharon had on a blue flower print dress, and her hair was pulled back and caught behind her neck with a silver barrette. She looked terrific. I was glad I had taken him seriously and worn a sports jacket myself.

We ate at an upscale Japanese restaurant in Mississauga, laughing at each other as we struggled with the little pointed chopsticks they give you.

"Why Japanese food?" I asked him, struggling with some whole-wheat noodles that tasted like seaweed and kept sliding from between my chopsticks. "I thought your favourite was Italian."

"Oh, just to set the mood," he said mysteriously. Sharon rolled her eyes.

After we left the restaurant, my father piloted the van onto the Queen Elizabeth Way.

"Hey," I pointed out, "you're taking the wrong ramp. This is westbound."

"Yeah, I know," he said, puffing great clouds of smoke into the air. "We're going to Hamilton Place."

"Oh, no," I moaned.

Sharon laughed. "Yep. *Madama Butterfly*."

Sure enough, there we were in centre orchestra, my father and I with Sharon between us, listening to the fat folks on stage blasting away in Italian even though they were all dressed up like Japanese *samurai* who had escaped from one of those medieval martial arts movies.

"I think I prefer Willie Nelson," Sharon said a few minutes into the opera.

"I think I would, too."

The story was about an American sailor who was stationed in Japan some time during the early 1900s, and who apparently had nothing better to do than stomp around and blare tunes at anybody who came near him. Instead of taking the opportunity while he was in Japan to hit the malls and pick up a cheap stereo or the latest computer, he put the move on this Japanese woman. In fact, from what I could gather, he sort of bought her and played house with her for a few months.

The woman fell in love with him, naturally, and just before he took off back to the States—he was probably sick of eating seaweed and rice balls and wanted to sink his teeth into some genuine California junk food—he promised her he'd return and they'd live happily ever after and blah, blah, blah, like that—the usual. Everybody except her knew he was leading her on.

You didn't have to be a genius to know this one was going to be a tear-jerker.

The heroine's name was Butterfly. Which was a major joke. First of all, in spite of the traditional clothing, she looked about as Japanese as a Big Mac. And her name didn't quite suit her. I mean, butterflies *flutter*. This woman lumbered around like a hippo, blaring at her maid every two minutes about how in love she was. Later she had a baby, so she warbled away at him a lot, too.

I suffered through most of the opera, fidgeting as the story unfolded, relieved when the intermission came. In the last act the sailor was visiting Japan with his American wife. Without knowing why, I just *knew* Butterball was going to lose her son. Then, I hate to admit it, I got kind of interested.

At one point, she was singing this pretty nice tune about how she never lost faith in the sailor, how she knew in her heart that their love was so powerful he would never forsake her, how all the pain and anguish of waiting for him, wondering where he was, what he was doing— all that would end, and things would work out okay.

And as she sang, even though all the circumstances were as different as they could be, I tuned right in to how she felt. Deep in the cellar of my memory the laser clicked on and I went into a Replay, seeing myself when I was seven, sitting in my room and looking at the postcards for the millionth time, wondering where my dad was, what he was doing, and full of ache because I didn't know why he had left me.

And I started to cry. Right there in the theatre, surrounded by sophisticated men and women with their expensive clothes on, I felt my throat tighten and the hot tears slipping down my cheeks. God, was I embarrassed!

I stole a glance at my father, only to find he was looking at me.

He was crying, too.

We looked at each other for a split second, then both of us burst out laughing. We were laughing and crying at the same time.

Throwing her fists out sideways, Sharon punched us both in the chest. "You guys," she said. Then she started to laugh.

We couldn't stop. The people in front turned and glared at us, shush-ing us. We were definitely ruining the mood, but we didn't care.

Afterword

Some readers may be surprised or incredulous that Jack Chandler was able to keep his secret so well, even from his wife and son. However, research makes it very clear that such cases are by no means rare. There are more than a few Jack Chandlers out there.

— W.E.B.

Acknowledgements

I would like to thank the following for their help in the writing of this book: for financial assistance, the Ontario Arts Council; for sharing his research, Charles Craig, director of Craig Reading and Educational Services, Inc.; for technical information on wrestling, Wayne Lennox, Peter Montroy, Jody Snider and Mike Kitchen; for support and encouragement, John Pearce; for inspiration, Brendan Bell; for advice on the story, Megan Bell and Dylan Bell; for copy-edit, Shaun Oakey; and as always, for her help in editing the manuscript, and especially for encouragement and emotional support, Ting Xing Ye.